THE JAVA TAVERN

Fangs & Fiends

Anniversary Edition

By

Elizabeth Garver

ISBN-13: 979-8768095932
ISBN-10: 1477123456

Cover design by: Pixel Studios
Library of Congress Control Number: 2018675309
Printed in the United States of America

This book is dedicated to:

My family and friends that have
supported me through this author journey.

Contents

Contents.. iv
From the Author............................. 1
1... 3
2... 9
3... 25
4... 37
5... 52
6... 72
7... 84
8... 98
9... 105
10... 119
11... 138
12... 148
13... 168
14... 183
15... 198
16... 204
17... 212
18... 216
19... 229
20... 235
21... 242
Epilogue.................................... 254
Check out other books by this Author!
.... 258
About the Author....................... 259

From the Author

Thank you for picking up the first installation of The Java Tavern Series! This has been quite the journey. I cannot thank you enough for your reviews, word of mouth and encouragement I've received through-out this author journey.

The first book I published was never meant to be anything beyond an ebook. With much prodding from my family and friends I was encouraged to publish the book as a paperback! If you saw the first version of Fangs & Fiends the formatting is horrible. I also didn't realize how many mistakes I had made through-out the manuscript. I didn't have a firm grip on Eliza and her friends at the time so this is my opportunity to tweak the character building in this book to match further developments deeper in the series.

I've learned a lot since publishing the two other books in the series and my writing style has matured. The storyline is the same but I have tweaked some editorial type approaches and fleshed out scenes for clarity. If you already have a copy of this book and you read them side by side, you'll be able to notice subtle changes along with a big sweeping change of articulation.

New Bern was a tough place to grow up. There still aren't many places' teenagers can go to just hang out and exist. If The Java Tavern was a real place, I like to think of it as the hub for all the town's teenagers to spend most of their spare time.

As an adult living in New Bern I am now appreciate the quiet, deep rooted history and spooky vibe that encompasses this town.

I hope to transport you to the parallel universe of a magic filled New Bern while still maintaining the deep ties to American history this sleepy colonial town is saturated in. Join me on this adventure with Eliza while she tells a story about her first solved murder case, complete with lively ghosts and hidden secrets in every corner.

1

The coffee shop had always been a dream of mine. I didn't realize it was going to be my end-of-life plan, but here we are. I grew up in this sleepy coastal town in North Carolina so it just made sense that I would open a spooky coffee house that had extra space available for paranormal investigators and tabletop gamers, alike, right?

I hated growing up here and never expected to live here again. Something about turning thirty changed things for me though. This little town started to shine under the street lights. I started to feel more comfortable in my own skin. I made a real friend. When this property became available, I knew I wanted to create a space that younger me would have thrived in.

My business is right on Middle Street, I get a lot of patrons in suits that just enjoy the coffee and baked goods at the counter on their way to their stuffy cubical job. I always wondered if they were nerds in a previous life and loved the aesthetic, or if the Tavern was just convenient in a boring routine way.

I have four employees and myself. We are a tight group for the most part. I do all the baking myself with occasional help from one of my weekend employees. Every morning I bake five different kinds of cookies, two different types of quiches, a few breakfast pastries, and my signature Baby Muffins.

The muffins are baked with an egg in the center of delicious savory bread. The bready muffin part has sage and sausage or bacon and maple syrup baked into it. These muffins had become what my coffee shop was known for. I am not a traditionally trained pastry chef.

When I entered the contests to help promote my business the cooking community was offensively shocked that I managed to create a menu item that is complex enough to win some regional awards.

I'd like to say we are a humble coffee shop but that just isn't the vibe. I hang my awards proudly around the establishment and keep my muffin recipe secret. There is a trick to my baking technique that can only be explained as magical.

I started this business with money my father had left me after he died. I don't want to hear any apologies about his death, I hated that fucker. The best thing he ever did was leave me money. Typically, I don't tell people where I got my money from to start this business. My mother has plenty of money so people assume she gave me a loan anyway.

Part of the thrill of opening such a niche coffee house was the possibility that it'd fail and I'd lose every dime that asshole gave me. To my glorious horror, my geeky coffee shop is now a staple tourist stop making every overpriced coffee being sold a silent sound of personal triumph.

Each staff member has their own distinct style. Lexi, my main barista goddess works the morning shifts Monday through Friday. I unapologetically poached Lexi from a chain coffee shop on the business side of town. Lexi stood out like a sore thumb with her polished trust-fund-baby face, soft blonde hair, and khaki pants. Everyone has to wear a screen-printed black tee-shirt with The Java Tavern logo, but I let their personality show with their choice of pants, shoes, and accessories. As long as they followed the health department guidelines for personal hygiene and had clean clothes, that is. I just let them be who they are.

A couple of nose rings and bright orange hair will not affect the taste of your coffee, I promise. My staff also were allowed to kick people out for any reason. I don't require anyone to wear a nametag for many reasons. I've never found a reason to side with the customer when there is a customer complaint either.

There is a prominent sign that says: *"The customer isn't always right here, so leave if you're an entitled jerk"* The sign really sets the mood when you walk up to the counter.

Lexi is the scariest of us all and she blends the most with the general populous. I've seen her silver tongue make a grown man in a three-piece suit cry and then subsequently apologize to another customer for his behavior before she'd serve him his double shot espresso.

Khai is my afternoon employee that works Monday through Friday. Khai moved here from Maine a few years back and was my first hire after Lexi. They are an experienced barista that plays a lot of Pathfinder during their off hours. Khai likes to talk about computer builds and other things I have no interest in but I can't help but want to listen to every word they say anyway.

Tiff, Khai's friend, was hired in as a mid-shift a few months ago and no one seems to like her. Me, especially. I may not like her due to her connection to Khai, but Lexi's distaste for Tiff just validates me begrudgingly tolerating her for Khai's sake. Tiff dressed what I describe as cutesy goth. She always has streaks of green or purple in her long black hair. Tiff has a bunch of piercings and tattoos but nothing about her feels authentic or extraordinary.

Gregor is my weekend everything master. He is the only front employee that I trust in the kitchen completely. He fills up a room with his boisterous jovial personality. Gregor pulls a double shift on Saturday after working Friday evening with Khai. This way I got Friday nights off and only did the baking on Saturdays. Tiff worked a short mid on Saturday to give Gregor a long lunch break. Greggy's personality is hard to explain, really. You'll just have to meet him in person to understand.

2

I was bent over putting the last batch of apple popovers in the display window when Lexi cleared her throat behind me. I turned to face her.

"Yes, Lex?" My expression confused.

"There are some uniforms here to see you, Eliza," She said, looking past me over the display with a concerned expression, "Chad is with them," She added curtly. No one particularly enjoyed being around Chad.

I groaned audibly and followed her gaze to the three uniformed officers. One of them, was in fact, my high school boyfriend Chad. You could never guess it now but Chad was once an angsty emo skater kid in the nineties. Now he's a law enforcer when we use to steal cigarettes at the local K-Mart, before it shut down. Back then smoking as a teenager made you appear edgy and cool. The

K-Mart probably shut down from all the local teenagers stealing, I guessed in hindsight.

Chad now stood with a matching uniform with the rest, only his youthful floppy blonde hair and blue eyes set him apart from the older darker-colored hair of his colleagues. His broad shoulders and sturdy frame filled his uniform nicely. You could look at him and know that he spends hours at the gym through-out the week.

"Hey, boys, free drip coffee and a scone all around?" I tried to lighten the mood. Chad looked like someone had kicked his puppy and the violent individual was me.

"Lizzy, we're here on business," Chad used my high school nickname lovingly but spoke curtly with a nod, "You have a minute? We can go outside?" He rotated his head around at the busy seating area and all of the faces turned towards them.

Soft jazz played from the ceiling speakers and all the front windows were open to let in the cool, early fall breeze. Even with full tables, my patrons spoke in hushed tones with each other as if we were in a library. The vibe is very chill and the only time it got noisy in here was on the weekends when the tabletop gamers took up most of the tables and something interesting had just happened to their mystical alternate personalities.

"There is a booth over there that will fit us all. Unless you plan on cuffing me, I don't see why we can't do this over free coffee? I never get to sit down this early in the day," Glancing down at my watch to see it was only eight in the morning.

The early morning rush had already wrapped up for the on-the-go office crowd and this was the lull before the brunch crowd. The surrounding businesses opened about two hours after I did if not later in the morning.

Phoebe, who ran the Pretty in Pink boutique next door, would be here any moment for our usual morning routine of coffee and whatever the pastry of the day was before she opened at nine o'clock.

This police business better be quick, I grumbled internally. I watched the officers all make eye contact without speaking. Chad shrugged. Without a word, they all migrated to the booth I had motioned to.

I grabbed a whole pot of coffee and grabbed four mugs with the other hand. Lexi plated six random pastries and walked behind me. Her face never stopped expressing worried glances as we walked. She put the plate of pastries down and two small pitchers of coffee creamers down before shooting me another glance.

"Thanks, Lex. We're good here. I'll call if we need anything else," I reassured her.

She smiled weakly but still hovered. My barista's loyalty went beyond just being a fantastic employee and it's moments like this that I could recognize this fact clearly.

"Really, Lex. Thank you," I said in a stern tone.

Lexi begrudgingly backed away to sit on the stool behind the counter to wait for a customer to walk through the door.

I casually poured everyone's first cup of coffee and explained the two creamers. I always offer regular half-and-half and a plant-based milk option. You could also buy a full pot of drip coffee here like a pitcher of margaritas. You'd be surprised how many people order an entire pot of coffee and will sit there for up to three hours drinking it all. I served the full pot of coffee in a plastic thermal carafe though, so us having the industrial glass carafe at the table felt weird to me.

"Lizzy, enough about the creamers. We're here because of Hammond Fletcher," He pulled a small notebook from his breast pocket and flipped through a few pages.

"Hammond Fletcher? Who is that?" My brain raced trying to place the name. Mentally I pushed down the irrational anxiety that was fighting its way to the surface.

"He, uh, went by a different name most likely. Gagnar maybe? Or Thorny?" Chad seemed confused by his own information.

His colleagues were eating pastries and drinking coffee like they were there on a social call, not even looking in our direction. Clearly, they had known where Chad was going and hoped the free food and coffee would happen. I tried not to nervously witch cackle as I climbed a nearby wall.

"Thorny? Yeah, I know that name. He's a funny kid. Has some social issues. He plays here on Thursdays with his Vampire LARP group. They're an interesting group. Couples only," I wiggled my eyebrows for emphasis, "They're just here for the foreplay before they go into whatever cave they came out of. I don't ask too many questions. I overhear enough things from them that I'd rather never think about ever again," I could feel my ears growing warm from embarrassment.

I may dress like it's Halloween all year but the way people throw around their personal sex lives in public spaces never appealed to me. I had told that group not to go into the bathroom in pairs a couple of different times. I couldn't afford to keep fixing broken sinks.

Suddenly the other officers weren't eating their pastries anymore and were interested in our conversation.

"When is the last time you saw this Thorny guy?" Chad said, flipping to a fresh page.

"Umm, I'm not sure. Today is Monday, right? So maybe Friday or Saturday? He was here for the usual Thursday LARP tea time deal they have reserved on Thursdays and he usually comes back during the weekend dressed like a regular human and gets an iced earl gray with extra honey and a shot of lavender."

"Anything else?" Chad said, not looking up at me.

"Oh uh... I think he grabbed a Baby Muffin with sage and sausage that day. That was definitely Saturday right before noon. Pheebs closed her shop early so we could rent kayaks at the place by Brice's Creek that day and I remember Tiff was running late so it was this whole thing." I said triumphantly, remembering clearly now.

"No," Chad said with a small chuckle, "I mean, was Mister Fletcher A-K-A Thorny with anyone? Did he seem anxious? Rushed? Did he say anything strange?"

I gently put the tips of my fingers to my lips and nervously bit my lip as I tried to recall seeing Thorny. We're pretty dead for lunch and dinner since we don't sell full meals. The Java Tavern is a strictly snack and beverage establishment. The brunch crowd overlaps a little but unless we have something special on the schedule the whole place is slow between ten in the morning to about one pm. Tiff loves to work that shift because she gets her college work done during the lull. My other staff avoids those hours because of the lack of tips. It works out for everyone.

"I'm sorry. All I can think about is Phoebe falling out of the kayak and us going to a concert in Jacksonville at that dive bar. I almost forgot that I had worked that day at all. Upfront, I mean. I haven't missed a day baking in this place since we opened. That's why we're closed on Sunday. I think I sleep twenty hours straight on Sundays. Just to start my week over at three in the morning on Monday. You know that," I added the last bit to embarrass him.

Like all high school romances in a small town, we had tried to restart the spark right after I moved back. The Java Tavern was just in the launch process and Chad helped me with some of the preliminary grunt work.

Our rekindled romance only lasted a couple of months and I don't think we spent one full sober night together so I hardly feel like it counts. It does help to have a police person in your corner, so we just decided to be friends until I had more time for romance. It's been more than three years ago now. I haven't made any room in my life for romance since then.

Officer Smith, according to his name tape, spit out his coffee back into his cup. I flashed my eyes at Chad who was now rolling his eyes at me.

"Where was the concert in Jacksonville? Who saw you there? Anyone other than Miss Kirkpatrick?" Chad said using his professional voice and purposely glazing over what I had insinuated. He even referred to Phoebe like he didn't know her. Chad had taken some notes while I spoke too. I was sensing that something serious had happened to the boy in question, and I might be a suspect.

"Drakon, um, Devon Tillman is a bartender at Hooligans, he's a regular here, he's the one that got us the concert tickets. He served us drinks all night," I sipped on my black coffee and wrapped my fingers around the mug, trying to pull the warmth from the ceramic, "Is Ida okay? I'm not sure what her real name is. Ida Finkle is the character she played in their role play game. I didn't think Ida and Thorny were a real thing outside of the role-playing world but again, I tried not to ask any questions with that group. They clearly were a kink geared game. I never saw Ida outside of the Tavern and if she came back as herself, I looked right past her. These people come in here in full garb, wigs, fang teeth clip-ins, colored contacts and all," My voice was a bit more serious now.

"She is a sweet girl though," I continued, "She seemed a little young for the group but I'm not open very late so I'm not officially a part of the bar scene or anything so she never got carded. The table never ordered any of the beers we have on tap and as far as I know, they just ate their cucumber sandwiches with their hot tea and tipped well. I always prepared two types of teas and they always leave once the tea runs out. About two hours, maybe. I caught the vibe that they finished the role play in a more private setting," I ended with a slight cringe.

I was just thankful they didn't destroy my bathrooms anymore. I couldn't exactly prove it was them but I replaced the baby changing station in each bathroom twice. My staff all thought it was that particular LARP group.

Chad leaned towards me. I was telling him new information, "This Ida. She about five four, maybe? Kind of curvy? Did she ever mention her real life outside of the role play?"

"Yeah, sure. That fits her. We don't wait on that table at all. Their leader, Lucius of Vania, placed the order and requested the food to be placed on the reserved table before their established time. He prepaid over the phone so he could be in character while here, I guess. They were never late so we use warming plates for the tea kettles and their snacks were always served cold. We just assembled the table within ten minutes to six and they arrive together in with a grand flourish entrance. They'd make a big show walking through to the back to the reservation room," I gestured to the small room without a door.

From where we sat you could see into the space that held an empty long table and chairs. I decorated it with books and old candle sconces with electronic candles. The room had a fake window created from a framed TV that we could change the subtly moving picture to help make you feel like you were in whatever fantasy world you wanted to portray. The TV was off if no one was renting the space. The room was free for anyone on a regular day, you just had to pay for a reserved time and the extra perks of the TV and simple snacks.

There is enough room for twelve people to either sit or stand comfortably around the large table. There is a printed schedule posted by the room door that just said "available for free play" or "reserved" and one behind the counter with group names and contact information for the Game Master. We had other space available too and some groups just used our Book Nook, which has a real fireplace and enough seating for six if the party squeezed in on the couch and utilized the large overstuffed lounging chairs. Some patrons would drag over wood chairs from tables into that space to accommodate their group too.

Last year was a great year financially so I was able to widen the space into the large seating capacity it is now. I finally feel established as I get into my fourth year of business. I can let my employees run the show most of the time. It feels like I'm just the baker that handles the paperwork for some unseen owner most days. It is jarring when I remember that I am the owner and none of this would exist without me.

The only time I stand behind the barista counter is to help through a rush or to cover a shift for someone. I do not like dealing with the general population as a personal rule. I don't know how my staff does it every day.

"Tell me more about Lucius of Vain-yah?" Chad said, scribbling in his notebook.

"He was older than everyone else, I think. Not by too much, around our age or a little older. The other people in the group were closer to Lucius's age but Thorny and Ida was an easy ten years younger than them. I may be wrong though. Dudes are kind of hard for me to gauge sometimes. Plus, the wigs and make-up," I shrugged, squeezing my coffee cup closer to my chest.

"I don't know his real name off the top of my head," I rambled on nervously, "I'm sure it's in his receipts in the computer somewhere. I'll pull that up for you and leave it under the register for you by tomorrow morning. It'll take me a minute though because he doesn't call ahead on any specific date or time before they arrive. I'll have to look through the last seven days before. They always order the same thing though so it should be easy to find the same dollar amount. They've rented that space for a little over a month. The bathroom issue was the only problem I had with them. They kept within the group while they were here. They also stayed in character through their entire time here."

"Thanks, Lizzy. This helps a lot." Chad said, standing up, "I'll text you if we end up not needing that name. I don't want you to waste too much of your day on this. You were our only lead and you've been a big help. Just don't leave town, okay?" The rest of the uniformed officers got up with Chad, shoving pastry into their mouths and taking the rest of their coffees like shots at a bar.

"Sure. Whatever you need," I stood up and pushed my sweaty palms down my apron front.

"What are these called?" The oldest appearing officer asked, holding up a large pastry he seemed to be taking with him.

"That's my apple popover. I add caramel to the apple mix before I bake it. It's delicious, right? Go see Lexi on your way out and she'll hook you up with a to-go cup and a free pastry of your choosing, fellas," I gave a big awkward smile to Chad, who seemed annoyed by how nice I was being to his coworkers. They quickly walked to the front. I stayed a quick step ahead of them.

"Give'em whatever they want on the house, Lex," I said as I buzzed by her. She rolled her eyes at me but I took that as acquiescence.

The small pack of officers left through the glass double doors. Phoebe was waiting on the sidewalk watching the parade of uniformed officers get to their vehicles.

She pushed her way into the dining area once the doorway was empty. Phoebe turned on her heels and stared out at the police officers without trying to be subtle. I joined her at the door. Together we looked out towards the now driving off police vehicles together.

"Was that Chad and his goon squad?" Phoebe asked, crossing her arms across her chest.

"Yeah, but he wasn't here for pleasure. I'm not exactly sure what happened but it has something to do with the creepy kink vamps that come here on Thursdays," I mimicked her body language and crossed my arms too.

"Did you make those apple things again?" She turned towards me, moving on from the cops.

"Sure did, I'll grab us some." I smile, happy to have a friend I could talk to about what just happened.

3

After breakfast with Phoebe, I went upstairs to my apartment above the coffee shop to turn on my laptop to see if I could find the information Chad was asking for. If I did it right now, I wouldn't antagonize over it or risk not having it done when he comes around again.

Since I didn't want it to seem like I was withholding any information I grabbed screengrabs off the cameras from the previous Thursday. The images were almost horrible after the printer was done with them but you could see the group in vampire garb and the timestamps were clear. I wrote "entering" and "exiting" on the appropriate images. I even grabbed a screenshot of Thorny at the front desk grabbing his coffee on Saturday around one in the afternoon wearing normal clothes.

Tiff had been a full hour late for her shift that day. I let it run at five times the speed as I watched him sit down at a booth by the front windows and long after I had left, he was still sitting there, staring out in front of him almost completely motionless. He had gotten his iced tea for there so he was drinking from a glass cup that had my logo etched into the side. We sold so many of those glasses to tourists, I mused, they were worth the investment.

Tiff had been propped up at the front desk with her laptop out and a thick textbook. She only took breaks from her book and laptop to wait on the few to-go customers. The young cutesy goth did a few walk-throughs of the front to make sure all the tables had been bussed and made herself an iced coffee with an extra shot of espresso.

At some point, I was so focused on Tiff that I missed Thorny getting up to leave and had to rewind until I got the time mark. He had sat there for nearly four hours nursing that one iced earl grey. By the time Tiff had packed up at four to go home, Khai came in to work the last five hours of the night. By then we had a table or two on the larger seating side playing some type of tabletop games and a few couples sitting on the barista counter side of the coffee house.

Tiff and Khai were an interesting pair. Khai had brought me Tiff on a silver platter and sacrificed their own hours to get her the job. I always wondered what their dynamic was.

Slowing the tape down to twice the speed I watched them chat. There was no audio on the video recording so I didn't bother trying to eavesdrop that way. I watched as Tiff subtly traced her finger along the neckline of Khai's shirt collar and how she tilted her head while she drank from her iced coffee.

They spoke for an easy thirty minutes before Tiff slowly walked out the door. Intrigue. I don't care if my employees date as long as it isn't a problem. To be honest, I was purely being nosey at this point. Just to be thorough I kicked up the speed again and finished out Khai's shift.

They are a great worker and handled their shift without issue. Khai even went the extra mile by waiting on the tabletop gamers. My employees are not waitstaff for customers so I don't require them to serve anyone at the tables.

The entire staff has learned that on slow nights if they give gamer tables just enough extra attention they'd make some extra tips by the end of the night, though. It didn't take much extra attention, either. You had to find the balance of not breaking their moment in-game but also inserting yourself in a helpful way that you may get an extra sale or two off of them. Offering to deliver whatever they order to the table helps with the tips too.

It took me until lunchtime to finish my snooping and research for Chad.

As I closed my laptop, I could feel my phone vibrating in my pocket. Phoebe wanted to meet for lunch. She suggested we go to the Italian place at the end of our street. Before I met up with Phoebe in front of her boutique, I checked in with Tiffany who was now on shift.

I tucked the manila folder of information under the register with a brief explanation that either Chad or a uniformed cop may swing by at some point retrieve it.

I texted Chad that the information he requested was already with my employee at the register. I propped myself with my shoulder against the outer wall of Phoebe's shop as I quickly typed the message.

An old man walked past me staring down at my phone and he loudly scoffed.

"Get a fucking job, loser," the old man huffed under his breath as he passed by.

I looked up and started laughing loudly. I just couldn't process the audacity of the older generation sometimes. He never slowed his stride as he kept walking but I couldn't get back to my message sending from the shock.

"How about you eat a dick old man!" I yelled after him. The old man turned towards me as Phoebe walked out of her shop looking at me then to the old man with a confused expression.

"Hi, Mister Byrum! Having a lovely day today, are we?" Phoebe broke the silence. He waved us off and turned back around to keep going where he was headed. My friend turned towards me and scolded me, "What did you do to piss him off?"

I shrugged, "He didn't like that I was propped up against your fine establishment while I texted my ex that I had the shit he needed, I guess. Who fucking knows?" I scratched my scalp behind my ear, it was a nervous tick I had developed since moving back to my hometown.

At lunch, I filled Phoebe in on all the recent drama that was unfolding around me. I also added the flirting between staff I discovered while I watching the security footage.

"Khai is kinda sexy. I can see it," Phoebe said as she sipped her margarita. That's why she wanted to come here. This upscale Italian eatery does a margarita drink special on Mondays starting at lunchtime.

I wasn't against the unexpected drink special choice. By this point, we both were finishing our second discounted beverage. Although now I was day drunk and it wasn't even two in the afternoon yet. I did most of the talking so as I got thirsty. I was consuming my margaritas too fast.

"You're just drunk," I laughed nervously, licking the salt from the rim of my now drained glass.

"You did the nasty with Khai, I knew it!" She was poking me in the shoulder now and I covered my face in shame. She had read my guilty expression plainly.

"Only that once and it was a mistake. We don't bring it up and they've never said anything other than asking if they still had a job," I could feel my ears burning.

"I mean, it was great but I can't be doing that with my employees," I stuttered out, "That's not something I want to be known for. Plus, they're way younger than me so it's probably some kind of creepy boss fantasy thing that happened anyway. No one can know," I insisted.

I waived to the cocktail waitress, if we're going to discuss this, I'm going to have to have another drink. The waitress brought over two more margaritas and a refill on our house breadsticks and marinara sauce. It was a strange mix but the alcohol was hitting me in a way that required more bread.

"Khai is only eight years younger than you. Khai's brain is fully developed as a twenty-seven-year-old adult. You make it sound like you're twenty years older and you offered to only pay them after they did things to you," Phoebe came to my defense, "I only say I'd take a turn because you don't seem very invested in them and any good friend shares the wealth when they can," Her giggles made me feel slightly better.

"Shhhh, you don't know who's listening right now," I said a little too loudly.

"Everyone talks around here and working downtown is like working at the fucking mall. All of these employees talk. I can't ruin anything if there is something between Tiff and Khai. It's my vanity for even wanting to know how serious they are. Khai and I still flirt a lot but it's not heavy or anything. We have clear boundaries. We only had that one conversation about it after it happened and that's been that." I said, sucking hard through my straw.

"And this is my last one. I'm going to have to go home and nap this off," I insisted, "I'm fucked if Chad stops by in uniform and I'm like this. It's been too long," I laughed too loud and covered my mouth with my hand. We were sloppy and I couldn't help but notice the dirty looks we were getting from the other tables.

"How long?" Phoebe put both elbows on the table and started playing with the straw in her drink, "I bet it's not longer than me."

"You were dating Dan, though?" I tried to quickly redirect this conversation from my questionable love life to her own.

"Fuck Dan! I mean, everyone else did, right?" my friend said while laughing but her laughter didn't sound very happy.

"Shit, Pheebs. You didn't tell me he cheated on you." I licked the side of my glass while I made eye contact with the bartender who dropped the glass they were polishing, sending it crashing to the floor. *I could attract someone if I really wanted to*, I told myself.

"Yep. He told me after five years of being together that he didn't want to set a date for marriage because his much younger sidepiece had turned serious and they had gotten to the point of wanting to move in together. The audacity! It's been almost two months ago now but the last time we took a tumble in the sheets was many months prior to all that. I just couldn't knowing that he was seeing someone else. I have been too ashamed to tell you it was more than him just not wanting to commit. He just didn't want to commit with me," Phoebe looked into her glass with sad eyes and drained the last bit of liquid from her festive shaped glass.

"Khai was my last anything. Chad and I hooked up right when I moved back five years ago and I think maybe a few booty calls since then but our last real time together was two Christmases ago. He was in between girlfriends and the lonely holiday stress got to me, I swear. Khai happened last year around this time. Maybe Thanksgiving? Right when it gets cold outside, I get lonely. How fucking basic is that," I sighed. *What happened to our good time?* I thought to myself, *I needed to get us in a better headspace.*

"I saw Barry the other day." I tried to lighten the mood with Barry, my ever-present spirit guide from the astral plane.

I have always been able to see spirits but Barry is the only one that spoke to me on the regular. He was some type of nobleman from the eighteen hundredths and best I could tell he hated being dead so he clung to me like a literal life raft. Barry was the only consistent partner in my life and sometimes I worried that's why I couldn't find a romance in the flesh. I've had some very lonely moments since moving back home, alright. I'm not proud of it.

"Barry? What's that colonizer up to lately?" Phoebe got up from her chair and pulled out enough money to cover both of us plus the tip and sat it on the table. We walked out together with our arms locked. It felt nice being held by someone else even if it was to hold each other up from our mid-day buzz.

"He has discovered his own grave in the Cedar Grove Cemetery and he wants me to leave him a wreath of 'ivy and lilacs, my sweet lady'" I tried my best to mimic his posh British accent, "So I guess we should swing by the florist on the way back. It is just across the street," We crossed the street after letting a car pass.

Together we pushed the door open bursting through the threshold of 'Jenna's Florist Creations' like a herd of elephants. Luckily there was no one in there but the frightened employee behind the counter. Mondays were slow for everyone after lunchtime, I guessed.

4

"How can I help you, ladies?" The cheery girl behind the counter asked us. I took us a moment to get our balance back and through all miracles didn't knock over an entire glass figurine display near the front door.

"We have to buy flowers for a dead British guy," Phoebe said, thumbing through the business cards on the desk. They were all the same business card but Phoebe liked to appear busy.

"Do you have fresh ivy and lilacs?" I tried to maintain my composure and appear more sober than I felt.

"Lilacs are out of season right now but I could arrange for them to get here. Is there a date of the funeral and place we could deliver these to?" The girl pulled out the ordering form and started writing down some basic information.

"Yeah, about three hundred years ago and Cedar Grove," Phoebe chuckled to herself just above a whisper as she rearranged all of the little bear statues on a display near the counter.

"Ignore her. I'll just pick it up and it's okay if it takes a while, there is no deadline. I own The Java Tavern just across the way," I said, motioning behind me without turning my head away from her.

The girls eyes grew large and she gripped the clipboard to her chest as if I had just given her the worst news of the year.

"You have a bad experience there?" I asked in response to her rigid body language, starting to sober up.

"No, uhh... not like that, no. Did you want a specific color of lilacs? How will these be arranged?" Clearly, this girl was uncomfortable all of a sudden. My curiosity was completely peaked. Phoebe even paused from her imaginary busy work.

"A traditional wreath. Add a pretty bow or something too, I guess. I don't care about the colors, order what you think will look pretty, and go for it," I paused as I heard

Barry have an opinion although he did not manifest himself, "Um, wait, he wants white. Sorry, no ribbon either, I guess."

I paused just long enough for her to write the information down before I leaned over the counter.

"Ida, is that you?" I spoke in a more hushed tone just in case there was someone else in the back that she may not want to know about her vampire kink show on Thursdays. Barry was sighing with agitation in my ear, *'took you long enough to figure that out,'* He was saying in my mind.

"My name is Caroline and I'd rather you never mention Ida or anything you've seen her do while you're in here, please," As Caroline slash Ida spoke each word became more forced and her teeth were gritting just barely getting the words out. *Aha! I am finding something out,* I thought.

"I had an interesting conversation with a man with a badge today concerning your... uhh, Thursday situation. The person you may be most familiar with out of the group? Yes, well, apparently something is going on with him in a serious way and I need to know more about it. When is the last time you saw him?" I tried to keep my voice down low but the alcohol was making my perceptions skewed. I hoped I didn't smell too much like tequila as I hovered close to Caroline's face.

"He is a strictly Thursday type of friend if you know what I mean," Caroline leaned back and nervously adjusted her button-down blouse before grabbing her phone.

"The last message I got from him was Friday night," She said, "He is allowed to call after nine o'clock on Friday and we discuss what happened the previous evening. Then he can't talk to me again until the following week on Wednesday when we discuss our tentative plans for Thursday of that week. See?" She held up the cellphone so I could see the time stamp saying that the last text message on their thread was asking if it was okay for him to call and her agreeing to it. Then Caroline showed me the call log of their phone conversation. They had only spoken for about twenty minutes. Twenty minutes is still a rather lengthy conversation. As she held up the phone that's when I noticed the engagement ring on her finger and I understood a bit more.

"He doesn't know," Caroline answered before I even asked, "My fiancé thinks I have a class at the community college that night and he lives on base so weekdays are hard for him to come to New Bern, anyway. I just... I'm not sure how it all happened. Ham came in here and he'd do this silly voice like he was a vampire and would buy a single red rose from me every day for two weeks straight. He asked me to grab a drink with him after the thirteenth rose purchase. After I closed up shop one afternoon, we had a beer at your place. Coffee houses are less pressure, ya know?"

"Ham told me about the LARP group and I guess he had always wanted to join but he never managed to get a plus one. Somewhere in my brain, it got twisted up that it wasn't cheating because we were different people when it was happening. You do know you host a LARP kink group, right?" Caroline sighed and flipped through her phone more to pictures of Hammond and her in full vampire garb.

In the pictures, she was wearing a dark wig and had bright red contacts in. Hammond is biting her neck and they both look very cozy and natural together.

"The cops told me that Hammond is missing and assumed dead. They stopped in before going to your place, I guess. I had just opened and I had to send my mom on a stupid errand to make sure she didn't overhear any of it. My mom is the owner of this place, I just work here. Ham was a great guy but he LARPs, ya know? He delivers pizza for a living and is five years older than me. In five years, I want to be married and pregnant with my second kid," Caroline bit her lip.

"You can't have lots of kids with a pizza delivery guy," She reasoned, "He was a good time but not a forever type of guy. He knew about my fiancé. He knew I had already set a date for the wedding and our fantasy could only last but so long. I was sure that he and Lilith had a thing going, anyway. She role-plays that her character hates Ida but I know in my gut that she is jealous that I get to end the evening with Ham. She's ancient compared to him, too! I don't get it. I don't know any of these people on a personal level, though. We only had the orgy once and that's when I found out that Lilith and Lucius are married in real life! They had taken a lot of pictures down around the house but they missed one in the room that Ham and I ended up in... after—"

"The orgy," Phoebe said, her complete attention on Caroline now, I could almost hear Phoebe cheering in her brain about the depth of gossip we were getting.

"Right. That. Well, the other two wanted to keep going but Ham said he wanted to save his actual climax for me. That I was his Lady and he had to make sure I got off a few more times too, he didn't want to share me anymore," Caroline was nervously picking at the edge of my order sheet and looking down at it to avoid eye contact with us.

I was startled by how much she just blurted out to me. She's kept this such a locked-down secret that once it started coming out of her mouth she couldn't hold back anymore.

"What the fuck do you put in that tea, Eliza? I think I need some. You said this group meets on Thursdays? Who do I talk to if I want to join?" Phoebe sounded so genuine about joining that I took a step back so I could turn my whole body in my friend's direction with a puzzled look on my face.

"We do take a little Ecstasy. Lilith French kisses everyone and we get it from her that way like an offering. That usually happens right as we sit down," Carolina sighed heavily as she spoke, "Lilith, I'm not sure what her real name is, stands at the threshold of that room in the back and that's how she greets us, with a kiss, as we file in to sit down," Caroline took a deep breath.

Phoebe and I shared a glance but braced ourselves for the waterfall of information Caroline was giving us.

"Wow! This feels great to get out! Kissing Lilith and how it made me feel was the only reason why I agreed to the orgy. I had never been with a woman and we're all very safe and I had to give them copies of being tested for everything and proof that I was on some form of birth control before I could join the group, you know. The more I think about it all the more I realize that I might not have feelings for Ham at all and it's just the sex that is making me feel a type of way," Caroline paused.

"The sex with everyone, really... I could never tell the police any of this," Caroline's eyes grew big again, "I just told them about going to your place on Thursdays and that I did have a romantic relationship with Hammond but Hammond only. The truth was that by the time the E hit us enough we would end up at the alley off of First Street and never make it to an actual bedroom. The alley only happened twice, though. Hammond always brought me back to his place regardless though except for orgy nights. On Orgy nights we were required to stay the full night and we'd all end up in a huge bed in the basement of the house and sleep naked so any further play could happen until the next morning. There were a lot of little rules like that but the orgasms were worth it. Sometimes I wish we met twice a week, to be honest," Caroline smiled her sweet smile at me and I felt completely dumbstruck. Caroline looked so wholesome she could be Lexi's twin with their matching long blonde hair and round faces.

I was learning entirely too much about her and the pack she ran with. I completely understood, though. Most of the attraction I had for Khai was that it had to be kept a secret, right? We had hooked up twice but the second time was right before we talked about our boundaries and expectations.

I couldn't help feeling attracted to Khai and Khai was very aware of my attraction to them. It was hard to split hairs on who was pushing who into a corner about an actual romance though when we were throwing each other around every chance we got.

Before actually doing the dirty, we had made it to second base a few times after the coffee shop had closed and I couldn't even tell you who kissed who first. No one could know about us and I'm okay with being someone's fantasy.

As far as I know, Khai was single at the time and I haven't had a steady relationship since I moved back five years ago. Chad would've been my closest attempt, I guess, and that crashed before it had a real chance to fly.

Khai and I haven't touched in many months at this point and now I know Tiff was to blame for that. It was all for the best, though, I tried to convince myself. Other than physical neediness I had broken that part of me that wanted to couple with someone.

I was rather proud of how emotionally stable I have gotten on my own. My ex always told me I'd amount to nothing and be nothing without her but I had an endless amount of proof to prove otherwise, I tried not to smile on the outside at my inner-revelation.

"Wait. You said he wasn't allowed to call you, right? Does that mean Hammond would come over instead? To the shop?" I remembered him staring out my front window in the security footage. He could easily see into this florist shop from where he was sitting in the Tavern. "When was the last time he came to see you?"

"Saturday night he rushed at me as I was locking up. I had stayed after closing to finish up some bouquets for a wedding. The order is using artificial flowers but with other projects we have this week and my school schedule," Caroline paused, "I knew that I needed to get them done and I wasn't coming out here on a Sunday. Robbie, my fiancé, was going to come to pick me up because my mom had driven me to work earlier in the day. He said he'd drive into town just in time to pick me up and he'd drive me back to his barracks since his roommates were gone for the weekend. I wouldn't be able to drive on base anyway. It was a nice night out so he wanted to drive the hour round trip."

"Oh shit. Hammond was waiting for you to come out of the shop," I said, realizing where she was going with this.

"Yep. He was there to profess his love for me, I guess. I couldn't get a word in before Robbie was coming around the corner and heard the bulk of what Ham had to say before they started punching each other. Robbie is a marine that runs PT five days a week and Ham is a skinny gamer guy. You've got to know how this ended," She said, full guilt in her voice, "And I felt like shit, ya know? Here Ham is getting his nose broken over something I did. Ham isn't attached to someone like I am, as far as I know. I was the one wronging Robbie, not Ham. Ham just ended up being a good time that I couldn't quit."

"Did anyone call the police?" Phoebe was so invested in this story.

"I think so. Probably. It was a Saturday night downtown! On Main Street! We have bars on each corner. The employees you had working at your place came out to see if Ham was okay and that's when Robbie told me to get into his car because he didn't want to do another weekend cleaning toilets with a toothbrush. I left with him and my heart hurts. I regret leaving. I should have stayed with Ham and dealt with it all. I've called Ham every hour since that happened. Robbie and I are rocky at best. We're supposed to think about all this for a week and then he'll tell me on Friday if we'll get married or if I'm going to die in the florist shop as my grandpa did," Caroline sighed heavily as she shifted her weight from one foot to the other.

"Someone died in here?!" Phoebe pulled back like there was a monster around the corner just waiting to lash out at her.

"No, not that I know of. I meant metaphorically. Jenna is my mom's name but her father named the business after her when they opened this place seventy years ago or whatever," Caroline wrote something on the back of a business card and handed it to me, "Look, this is Ham's number. I consider this an emergency. You try to call him too. My number is the mobile number on this card. Call me if you hear anything too. He was also my connection to the others so I don't even know how to get up with them. We tried not to know anything about each other's real lives, for obvious reasons," Caroline did a few cleansing breaths.

"Look, I'm just going to do the wreath on the house and I'll drop it by on a morning I know you're still there, okay?" Caroline said with a smile, "Give me three or four days and I'll have this done for you. You've helped me process some stuff. I owe you."

I took the card and Phoebe forced Caroline into a hug. I swear Phoebe asked again how to get into the kink vampire group and I just tried to act like I didn't hear it. I waited for Phoebe outside while I stared at the entrance of my business across the street.

I looked at the florist shop door to read the store hours: Monday through Saturday open eight am to six pm. I put him leaving my place around five o'clock. I wonder if she was working late on her vampire lover and not those bouquets after all? Why would she tell us all of that personal stuff just to leave out the real timeline? We weren't getting the full story.

5

"Back to the grind, friend." Phoebe sighed as she came out of the florist shop and hooked arms with me again, "Do you think Barry knew? That's why he told you to get the wreath?"

"It honestly wouldn't surprise me," I shrugged, "He had told me about finding his grave last night and voluntold me to put the wreath on his headstone. He likes to play games sometimes. He might have known that the cops would show up at my place today, I guess? He looks out for me in ways I'll probably never understand until I'm on the other side with him."

We talked as we took the short walk across the street to our neighboring businesses. We had spent an hour at the florist place and it was nearly four o'clock. Khai and Tiff should be on shift when I came back. Normally I don't have two people on staff because I am the second person on staff.

Mondays are so slow I started doing a "Flash Sale" of our pastries and baked goods in bulk. Between four and six in the afternoon, we sell everything in packs of six, twelve, and twenty-four at half price. A lot of people come and stock up.

Khai and Tiff handle the crowds of people getting to-go pastries while I bus the tables and start on prep work in the back for the next day. Tiff would leave by six when the rush slows down and then it's just Khai and me until closing. Four evenings a week we closed the coffee shop down together, which is probably how the accidental not-romance got started. It was all so cliché I didn't like to think about the entire situation as a whole.

"Why did we have to talk about romance at lunch? Now I'm sad and horny. It's boring being hetero sometimes," Phoebe sighed and sat at the park bench beside her business.

"I don't want to adult anymore today," She whined, "Let's go up to your apartment and pretend like we have no responsibilities today, shall we? Or maybe get me drunk enough I'll take advantage of you? All this sex talk is making me itchy."

"As much as I'd love to take you up on that offer, I have to make my cookie doughs to put in the fridge. I ran out this morning. I should have gotten a delivery today of dairy stuff and when I'm not there to get it whoever let the delivery guy in just wheels it into my walk-in and doesn't put any of it away. It's my fault for leaving them alone all day today." I struggled with resisting Phoebe sometimes.

I never knew if she was actually sexually curious or if she just enjoyed torturing me. Phoebe was gorgeous and always wore soft flowy materials that made her appear as if she just strolled off a sailboat or a yuppie magazine. Her large stone necklaces and flowy scarves made her seem older than she was. At the core of it I knew I resisted her because I didn't want to mess up our solid friendship.

I was pushing forty and she fifty but neither of us felt the need to fit into what society told us how to be. That's why we worked so well as friends. Phoebe could blend better in this town than I could by appearance alone. Over this past year, Phoebe's gotten me to open up to her and she forced me to be her friend and I'm so grateful she did.

"Okay, fine. Just leave me here to die alone," Phoebe sighed dramatically while getting to her feed. She staggered to her boutique door like a zombie, "It'll just be me and Marleigh over here bored to tears because my friend would rather work her life away. Hey, maybe Marleigh will be my lover? How do I ask her without her quitting on me?" Phoebe laughed but her joke was not funny to me. Marleigh was almost half of our age, which was probably the butt of the joke Phoebe was trying to make.

"You aren't right," I laughed, "Bye, friend. Love you! Smoochies!" I tried to do my best valley girl impression and Phoebe rolled her eyes at me as she disappeared into her boutique.

I peered in and saw Marleigh, her teenage employee who works after school, flipping through a fashion magazine, perched on the desk beside the register. Marleigh barely looked up when Phoebe walked in to greet her. I didn't know who to feel sadder for.

I sucked in a deep breath and pushed through the Tavern door noticing the Flash Sale sign was already up outside. We had a few people tapping away at their laptops on the barista side and a small tabletop group in the book nook but otherwise, it was the quiet before the storm.

Tiff had been standing very close to Khai when I came in. I tried not to let it bother me. The only claim I had on Khai was being their boss and nothing else. Tiff told me that Chad had stopped by and that he wanted her to tell me to answer my messages. I had missed a few of his calls, she informed me. Khai gave no hint of possible jealousy and why should they be with Tiff right there?

I told them both that I would do a walk around and see if anything needed attention and then I'd be in the back if they needed me.

Only a few napkins needed replacing and a few sugar packets were sparse on some tables. I finally remembered to look at my phone by the time I made it to the back and pulled out all the ingredients for my base dough for the cookies I made in bulk.

I tried to do about twenty pounds of each type of cookie each week so they would last me most of the week without too much extra time spent while I did the more complicated pastries the next morning.

I felt my phone vibrate in my pocket so I pulled it out and looked at the screen. Chad was calling and I had luckily remembered my Bluetooth earbuds so I answered hands-free and put my phone back in my pocket.

"Yessir?" I said in a stern voice.

"Hey babe, I got your paperwork and you're thorough as always. My bosses were mighty happy about it. You happen to have those clips available on a thumb drive I can grab?"

"Umm, I don't think I have a thumb drive but I did save them to a separate file because I did not want to look for them again if you asked. Security camera shit takes too much time out of my day. Can't have a business without them, though. Did you call me 'babe'? You and Jessica split?" I loaded up the ingredients to my industrial mixer and let it go.

I would separate the dough into three parts and add in the extra nuts and chocolate bits. I decided to go with classic chocolate chip, double chocolate chunk, and white chocolate macadamia for the next week. Sometime this week I'd make another batch of snickerdoodles but it wouldn't happen today.

"She's old news. I broke it off with her months ago," Chad said flirting with me turning my stomach into knots.

He went on to say, "I'm sorry about how I was today. My partner was there and then those other guys just saw us park in the street and wanted to tag along because they love your coffee and cookies. You know I bring them into work all the time. Ah, anyway, I could bring the thumb drive over around nine tonight?"

"Well, I have a lot of prep work to do tonight. I'm making eighty pounds of cookie dough right now and have three other doughs I need to prep before morning. I'll be asleep before nine. Wait, if I'm a suspect or whatever shouldn't you be avoiding me or something? Business only?" I honestly had mixed feelings about hooking up with Chad again. He was a fun time and I did need a distraction but the baggage that always comes with his bullshit just didn't feel worth it anymore. Not to mention the guilt. Chad was an easy lay but being his dirty little secret wasn't always fun.

"Fine, be like that," He said in a playful huff, "I guess I could just swing by on my way to work tomorrow morning. I'll grab cookies for the guys and bring a thumb drive to put those files on. If you bring your laptop downstairs, I'll play nice. If you make me come to your apartment all promises are off," He laughed through my headphones.

I bit my lip almost until it bled, he knew me way too well.

"Well, I'll decide by tomorrow, okay? Either way: I'm not completely opposed to the attention. Just so we're on the same page here," I held my breath, that was already too much for Chad to take and run with. He liked the chase but got way too sensitive if he was being turned down.

His sensitivity was one of his major flaws and the reason why we never stayed consistent with each other. He didn't feel like men should have emotions while simultaneously throw the biggest toddler tantrum if someone hurt his feelings. It was in my best interest to tread lightly with him.

"Heard, babe. I get it. Tomorrow night is trivia, right? I'm not the main on the nerd boy case so I should get out early enough to take you out after trivia. Raleigh has shown up so I'm pretty much just the go-for now. I'm not high enough on the rungs to get clout cases. Hey, you should ask Harry if he's seen any new ghost pals lately," Chad chuckled to himself.

My nose scrunched up in disgust that I would be physically attracted to someone who speaks like this. Chad was about to talk me out of any hanky-panky with him before it even started.

"Look, you can't talk like that and expect any late nights, Chad. If we fuck it'll be on my terms and when I fucking say so. A kid may be dead and you're making jokes? It's Barry, by the way, not Harry, and instead of making fun of everything you may want to try and get some resources together so you can get that clout you need," I was fuming. I forcefully pushed my balled-up hands into the dough I had just put into its container leaving the imprint of my fists on top. I slammed the lid on it for extra dramatics.

"Whatever, babe. We'll see how you feel tomorrow when I'm pushing you against the wall and biting your neck since you like vampires so much," Chad said in his best seductive voice before the call disconnected. He had hung up on me.

We were thirty-five years old and we interacted like the teenagers we use to be so often when we got together. I think that was part of the appeal, if I'm being honest with myself. The yank and tug of questionable love choices as a risk-less teenager.

I was his secret through most of the high school years. Mister Football Star couldn't be known for hooking up with the lesbian gothy hurtle jumper from track and field, could he? Old habits never die, I guess. The secret worked out both ways, though.

My high school friends were mortified when the secret love affair came out right before graduation. Although Chad had brought Fiona Williams to prom, he had ended up meeting up with me during the early hours of the morning after his date refused him.

I tried not to ask too many questions when I didn't want to face the answers head-on. The girl I was dating was keeping me a secret too and I guess I felt like I was justifying some wrong by cheating on her. High school romance was not a rollercoaster I cared to jump back on.

I whipped around to put the big buckets of dough into one of the industrial fridges just in time to see Khai standing at the kitchen doorway holding the business phone in their hand.

"Hey Eliza," Khai said awkwardly, "your mom is on the phone. Don't worry, it's muted."

"Oh fuck, how much did you hear?" I asked, ripping out one of my earbuds and suddenly feeling like the weak sixteen-year-old I once was, the distress was clear on my face.

"Something about not fucking Chad unless it was on your terms. I didn't know you were fucking a cop," Khai's eyebrows were almost completely disappearing into their hairline, this was the jealousy I wanted to see earlier, "I didn't know that you and Chad were a thing. For how long?"

"It's complicated. He and I are *not* a thing. We fucked a lot in high school and well, some in adulthood too. Not recently, though. Not after we umm... well, you were the one helping me derail the Chad train-wreck but that shit didn't go very well either, as you know. My whole life is a fucking dumpster fire. You know this. Now give me the phone," I reached for it and Khai pulled the phone back so I had to step even closer.

This is not how today was supposed to go. Khai was just tall enough that their long arms made it hard for me to easily reach the phone from where I was. Khai smiled around the edges of their mouth pleased by my struggle.

"What are you doing?" I said aloud inching dangerously close to them mid-reach to the phone. Our faces were hovering so close I could smell Khai's sandalwood cologne.

"I just have questions that demand answers, is all. But later. Now you need to tell Barb what your plans are this weekend, she was saying something about a garden party at her house," Khai placed the phone in my hand but pulled me close into their chest once our fingers touched.

Khai's face very gently touched the back of my hand to their lips so I could feel their breath on my skin. We locked eyes and my heart lodged its self in my throat. It wasn't quite a kiss to my hand but a graze from their lips to the back of my hand. It was an extremely intimate gesture that barely lasted longer than a few seconds.

A small grunt or grumble escaped Khai's lips before they released my fingers from their grip. I blinked twice realizing I had been left there clutching the phone feeling suddenly flushed. I was standing all alone like the moment had never happened at all.

Begrudgingly, I pressed the mute button on the phone mustering my best perky tone.

"Hi, Mom. What's up?" Hearing this tone in my voice felt strange. My heart was still thumping in my chest. Why did Khai have to toy with my emotions like this?

"Oh really, dear. Must you address me like that?" My mother said disapprovingly. She is always so proper, "I'll make it quick since I called you on your business line. I need you here on Saturday to help with the catering side of my garden party. If you could bring me two hundred of your red velvet cookies, they'd just be divine with our fireside whiskey beverage we have planned after the actual dinner. I can send someone to pick them up earlier in the day but I need you here by six, dear. I'll see you then."

I tried my best to get a word in but my mom had once again agreed for me to feed her friends without my consent. I was mid-sentence when I realized the line had gone dead. It was her style to make requests and avoid a chance for me to say no. I was forced into the obligation.

Barbara Woods is probably why we have so many suits in here ordering coffees and pastries before they go to their stiff office jobs. I know my mom means well and it's been nice that for once in my life she's proud of me for my success.

I just wish her being proud meant I could blissfully avoid all of her fancy friends and not be the black stain on every event she has. No matter how well I think I prepared myself or underdress myself I still feel like I stick out like a sore thumb.

Phoebe and I met because I was shopping at her boutique for one of my mother's events last year so I owe my mother more than just giving me life. My mother unwittingly arranged for me to meet my best friend at a time that I needed a friend the most.

I didn't bring the phone back out front while I finished up the cookie doughs and a base dough for some of my pastries that would cold rise overnight. Luckily, we didn't get many calls this time of day so it didn't ring at all while I kept it hostage for the next two hours or so.

I finally came to the front of the store when I thought it was safe that Tiff had left for the evening. To my surprise, she was sitting at the table closest to the barista counter with Khai propped on the customer side talking to her. They were both full of giggles. Before they noticed me, I glanced around the dining areas to a nearly dead coffee house.

"Well, I'm going to head upstairs for the night. No need to be down here if we don't have any customers. Catch you all later," It was a weak move but I had enough excitement for the day.

I quickly moved towards the front door but paused when I felt Khai's hand on my shoulder. I turned my body towards them so we were facing each other completely. I could see Tiff out of the corner of my eye but I focused on Khai.

"Let's talk later. I'll come up after closing?" They asked in a hushed tone, their hand was still on my shoulder. I feel the warmth coming from their hand. Khai was purposely getting into my personal space, their hand slid down my arm until our fingers loosely laced together. I liked it.

I tried my best not to smirk as I glanced past Khai's tall frame to see a confused look on Tiff's face. I really shouldn't enjoy this as much as I do, especially since I could lose an employee over all this.

I have thought about it though and we don't have the space for Tiff as it is, which is why she has been on the shit shift since she started. Lexi hated her and Gregor avoided Tiff when he could, they were both equally angry every time I posted a new schedule with Tiff still on it. Business was better, but not stable enough for two employees on the payroll during one full shift good.

My eyes adjusted back on Khai's caramel brown eyes before I spoke.

"Sure. Come see me after you close up," I resisted the urge to lean into a kiss before I left for good measure.

Instead, I gently released their hand from mine. After the glass door shut behind me, I did steal one last look inside. Tiff's expression was red with anger. She stood quickly pointing towards the door in my direction. I glanced around the dining area and was glad that only one customer was left and they were wearing headphones gently bobbing their head to whatever music they were listening to. The customer was completely unaware of the argument happening behind them.

I had about an hour before Khai would come up so I rushed upstairs to my apartment and showered. After thoughtful consideration I put on a loose linen dress instead of pajamas. I put on my fluffy slipper socks because the autumn chill was setting in and my hardwood floors were bitter cold.

For extra courage I made myself a boozy hot chocolate. I sat on the couch and turned my TV on so I could pretend that I wasn't waiting anxiously for a knock on my door. I found an old cold case docuseries on one of my streaming services and tried to focus on the evidence of the case being presented to me. By the time the cold case was solved, there was a soft knock on my door and I casually got up, grabbing my empty mug from the coffee table on my way to the door.

"Hi, beautiful." Khai said, holding up a bottle of tequila, "You look absolutely smash-worthy tonight."

"Are you talking to me or the tequila?" I tried to steady my breathing so I didn't seem too desperate. Khai is a very fit twenty-seven-year-old, they had changed out of the Java Tavern shirt into a soft flannel top that was unbuttoned to expose the screen-printed band tank that was under it. A black linen scarf that had tiny flecks of glitter in it completed the look. They had reapplied some makeup around their eyes and I was realizing how much extra effort was taken just for me. I was beyond flattered and I was in the mood to make some bad decisions.

"To you. May I kiss you now or are you going to torture me?" Khai took a big step into the apartment and closed the door behind them without turning away from me. Khai reached over and put the tequila on the kitchen table that was behind me, making sure to lean as close as possible to me as they did so.

"Can you kiss me and let me still do some torturing?" I asked nearly panting from anticipation.

Without hesitation from Khai our mouths collided and before I knew it my alarm was going off the next morning. Khai was still here with my comforter barely covering their nakedness.

My first alarm goes off at three in the morning long before the sun rises even in the summer. Luckily, we live in an area that doesn't get a real winter or it would be even harder to get out of bed. Today, I managed to sleep in until my fifth alarm went off at three thirty-five. My body did not want to move and I had to untangle our legs before I could edge myself out from under Khai's slumbering body.

We never even got into the tequila, it greeted me on the kitchen table as I slowly walked into the kitchen. I debated on making a pot of coffee but I knew I was running so far behind that it would make more sense if I just showered before going downstairs and brewed a pot while I started the morning baking.

6

Well, telling Chad to fuck off will be easy today, I thought. I made sure to grab my laptop and left a note for Khai to come down for breakfast whenever they were ready or to treat themselves to the little amount of food I have in the apartment.

I primarily eat from the coffee shop or one of the restaurants a few steps away from my apartment. I've gotten so spoiled living downtown that whenever I need to use my car it required me to ask someone to jump the battery. I don't do big catering events or anything so when people request a catering-sized order, the customer has to come here to pick it up. I kept it simple that way to keep costs down.

I carefully walked down the small stairwell that led to the outer door. I unlocked the door to let myself out listening for the door to automatically lock behind me. I loved having an electric lock. I have an app on my cellphone that logged every unlock and attempt at the keypad. I could set up guest codes that expired too.

Khai had a code that I hadn't set to expire. Some of our make-out sessions had occurred in my living room after work hours. That's the closest I've gotten to commitment in five years compiled with the fact that I left Khai in my apartment unaccompanied just now. I was giving a serious amount of trust and I wondered how it'd be ruined for me.

I was done baking all of the cookies and halfway through filling all of the cream cheese Danishes when I heard the abrupt knock on the employee door in the back. I wiped my hands on my apron and slowly opened the door a crack before seeing Chad's smiling face on the other side. I opened the door all the way so he could walk in.

"I figured you couldn't hear me if I went to the customer entrance," Chad was in full uniform and the attraction I had for him the previous day had worn off. At least my bad decisions had some good side effects, I decided.

"You guessed right. The laptop is over there. I'll pull up the files for you. I still have a lot of work to do if I'm going to get all of this done by eight o'clock," I tried to meet his flirty tone but my words fell flat.

"How boring," He groaned, pulling on his thick outer vest, "Here is the thumb drive," He handed the small flat device to me and we walked over to the laptop together.

We didn't speak much while I transferred the files over and he stood nearly on top of me but I wasn't taking the bait. I was a serviced woman so I didn't need his scraps, after all.

Khai did not speak at all to me much at any point last night other than lover's phrases and things I know I wanted to hear. It may be complicated with Khai but that type of complicated didn't make me feel horrible like Chad did. I handed back the thumb drive and Chad took it back but made sure he partially held my hand to get it. I did not miss the gesture but I didn't acknowledge it either.

"You going to get my cookies and coffee for me?" He seemed a little sad that I wasn't playing cat and mouse today.

"Lexi is here already. She can help you. I already got her to box them up for you after I brought them out this morning. I'm running a little behind this morning, I overslept. This weather change is killing me. I am obsessed with Autumn and all but I could do without the freezing temperatures," I hoped he didn't ask me to elaborate and I hoped Khai wasn't upfront when I walked Chad out there.

To my relief, Khai was nowhere to be found and Lexi was happily handling the growing line of customers. This always happened when the weather turned cold. Everyone needed some type of warmth and comfort on those suddenly cold mornings.

I was not a barista when I opened this business so I had hired one of my friends to do the coffee side. When my friend had to move, we courted Lexi for weeks before she accepted my job offer. Lexi is my only full-time employee. My friend had taught me the basics but I'm slow as hell. Lexi is a thunderstorm when there is a big line. Honestly, I think I get in her way if I try to help brew with her. Instead, if I step in to help in the mornings, I focus on taking orders and dealing with the register only. I can make and pour dripped coffee and that's the best I can do, consistently.

"Lex, here is Chad," I said to Lexi's back. She looked at me quickly to acknowledge she was listening but didn't stop moving to fill orders, "Do you need help? I'm on my last pastry. I've got about five minutes left in this batch if you want me to jump in after I get it out of the oven?"

"Sure, Boss, that'd actually be great. I'll take care of him. Just come out here to get me through the next twenty or so minutes, then I should be okay," Lexi didn't even look in my direction while she answered me, her hands working the steamer and pushing the button on the espresso grinder simultaneously. She was amazing to watch and worth every penny I pay her for being here.

I gave Chad a quick squeeze on the arm and went to pull the Danishes out of the oven to cool while I helped Lexi out upfront. By the time I came out front again Khai was already taking someone's order at the register while Lexi seemed to do a ballerina dance behind him. Khai only stepped away from the cash register to pour a dripped coffee or to bag up to-go sweets. Chad was nowhere in sight.

"I don't know why Khai is here but I'm not complaining," Lexi said after she noticed me standing there in my dirty apron, "This line is getting out of hand for a Tuesday. When I had to warm my car up this morning, I could feel the rush of the morning in my veins already," She grinned from ear to ear.

"You truly are frightening, Lexi," I said in my most endearing voice. I walked over to Khai and they smiled at me because our secret was somehow so loud between us, "I was about to help her, you don't have to work two shifts."

He finished his transaction with the customer before turning to me.

"I got this, El. Don't worry about it. I'll just help her through this rush and then I'll come back there to talk. I'm taking my breakfast on the house, though," Khai was wearing the same street clothes from last night but the customers didn't seem to care, they just wanted the line to keep moving.

I felt a little guilty about not helping through a big rush so I walked the dining area and checked on the people who were seated.

Everyone was having a good time and even some of the regular customers in the back of the never-ending line didn't seem too annoyed by their extra wait time. Once I felt confident that Khai and Lexi weren't going to curse my name for abandoning them, I went back to finishing the pastries.

I made a few trips to the front to put up pastries but for how fast the displays were going bare I ended up back in the kitchen making more cookies and Baby muffins. I typically only made double batches of those on Fridays and Saturdays. To make them on a Tuesday just seemed strange and exciting.

I might have to hire an assistant baker if this keeps up. Honestly, I had been needing an assistant baker since I opened but I always seemed to make do without one. I had trained Gregor the most in the kitchen but he was still front-of-house staff per his job description. Gregor was in his early twenties and unsure what to do with his future. He has no interest in college and is still testing the water of his endless possibilities. As of right now Gregor worked somewhere else during the week without a hint of wanting to quit there to help me bake full time.

Lexi was my front-of-house manager although she didn't officially have that title. Khai's future here had always been a wild card and Tiff was barely working twelve hours a week.

I brought out the second batch of Baby Muffins right as the last one had sold.

I pulled the second batch of chocolate chip cookies out of the oven and sat them on the counter to rest before going on the serving pan. I turned around to see Khai standing patiently behind me.

"I just had to wait for you to set the hot thing down," Khai said before their mouth was back on mine. I gladly kissed back with full passion. After a few long moments, we came up for air.

"Thank you for not kicking me out when your alarm went off. I don't know if I could have even made it down the stairs so early in the morning after the torture and the pain you put me through last night," Khai kept me pulled close although I was getting flour all over their front from my dirty apron.

"I... uhh... that was a big thing for me, actually. I have never left anyone in that apartment alone before. That was a big trust move for me. You didn't steal all my toilet paper or break all my dishes, did you?" I tried to light-heartedly laugh but the fear was too real for me.

"What the fuck kind of people have you been with before?" Khai seemed a little angry but not personally offended, "El, just let me love you, okay? I'm adult enough to handle the business shit like we aren't a thing but when I'm clocked out, I want to tell people you're my... well, whatever you want me to call you, girlfriend? Lover? Significant other? I want to discuss terms with you and you've always been so careful with my pronouns I want to do this right with you."

I just stood there with my mouth hanging open as they spoke. I've only had one other person profess their love to me and she destroyed my world and then lit all of my belongings on fire after *she* cheated on *me*! We had dated and lived together for four years before I moved back to New Bern.

I thought we would be forever but then one of her little side pieces decided she didn't want to be a part-time lover anymore and dropped in on me at work causing a big enough scene that got me fired on the spot. From that moment on it was a quick downward spiral that landed me back in this sleepy coastal town. Instead of accepting defeat I have created my own safe space in this historical town in North Carolina.

"Did I just make a complete ass out of myself?" Khai began to ramble on after I remained silent, "I really thought I was reading your vibes right and then last night... I called it off with Tiff, I half expect her to flake on her shift today, to be honest. I felt like she was using me for a job anyway. She's a bit too young for me anyway," Khai realized what was just said and quickly spat out their next words in a rush.

"I mean, I know that we have an age gap and it doesn't bother me but we can both agree that there is a big maturity jump from twenty-one and nearly thirty. You're thirty-something, right? I feel like we've talked about ages before." Khai's eyes were big with concern.

I lifted my hand to Khai's mouth to gently shush them before I spoke.

"Look. I'm all for whatever our fucking means, okay? Let's just leave it at that right now. My ex truly fucked with my head so I am not even sure what I have to offer you," I lowered my hand and smiled reassuringly, "I'm here for the good things and if we can manage through the bad things on the other side of whatever this is, we can discuss terms, okay? Boundaries are a big thing for you so I'm open to ground rules. I just can't do this right now in my kitchen, while I'm covered in butter and flour, okay? So, let's just say that we're more than friends; only boss and employee during working hours... and I won't fuck anyone else if you won't?"

Khai shoved a hand out in between us and we shook hands. *How work appropriate,* I thought.

"Agreed, easily. Yes." Khai said a little too quickly with an awkward giggle. I noted the enthusiasm.

As we were shaking hands Lexi poked her head in through the door looking like she had seen a ghost and said, "Uh, Boss, you're going to want to see this."

7

"I didn't know if you wanted me to call 911 or your cop friend so I just got you," Lexi said between big gulping breaths, "I came out here to throw the trash out because the rush filled up both of the trash cans and the street can! You know the city doesn't dump those as they should. Well, anyway. I came out here with all three because you guys seemed pretty involved in your conversation. They weren't that heavy just awkward—"

"Lexi." Khai and I both said at once.

"Sorry, sorry. I threw the first one in and it exploded everywhere because I'm short and I don't like climbing on these things and the side door is like rusted shut or whatever. Luckily most of it landed in the dumpster but I was a good employee and cleaned up my mess and had to touch the damn dumpster anyway. That's when I saw, when I saw... well... I ran to you. Do you think it's that missing kid?" Lexi was heaving deep breaths and I could tell she was in the beginning stages of shock. Khai was standing beside Lexi with an arm around her in a comforting way.

"I believe you. I also believe our morning just got extra fucked but not in a fun way," I spoke calmly but internally blood was rushing in my ears.

I had to look. I knew that I needed to before I made any phone calls. I stepped on the edge of our dumpster and hefted myself up to peer over the side. I'm decently tall so I didn't have to strain to look over the edge and there was a very obvious leg, foot, and most of an arm sticking out of the top of the rubbish. It was hard to tell how long it could have been in there but the skin was not a natural coloring and the bugs were insane for how cold it was outside.

I carefully climbed down from the dumpster and looked at Lexi standing beside Khai.

"That is definitely a person," I said with a little squeak in my voice, "You two go inside like I said and I'll call someone."

I told Lexi not to leave because I know the cops would want her statement. I debated on closing up but I didn't want to lose a day of sales even though I'm sure we had already surpassed our usual Tuesday. Even with trivia in the evenings we still barely broke even in the afternoons early in the week.

It took ten very long minutes of me babysitting my dumpster with a dead person in it before the first set of flashing lights showed up.

"Who found the body?" An officer I had never met before asked me again.

"Lexi did. I told you that three times already. Did you get her statement yet or are you just burning my daylight asking me questions like a parrot with a new phrase?" I did not look scary enough to deal with this shit.

This morning I had overslept so much that I had only managed to put my hair up into two buns above my ears, put a leather leash choker on and I had managed to put on some black lipstick only because I couldn't find my emergency lip balm that was usually in my work desk this morning. It felt silly to only wear lipstick as my makeup but it was all I had. I know I looked like I was coming down with a cold to everyone else who is used to seeing me with my full-painted mask on.

"She's fine, Doug. I'll take the rest of her statement." Chad came to my rescue.

I knew I would owe him for this somehow but I had to walk on eggshells with him as it was. He guided me away from Officer Doug as if we were moving with a purpose.

"I met the reason why you blew me off this morning. I'm unamused." He casually said before pushing the door open to my fully packed coffee house.

Tiff had not shown up for her shift as expected so Khai was still working the counter. Lexi felt up to working after all because she was refilling sugar packet containers and paper towels, the expression on her face was more anger than being upset.

"Do you need me or my staff for anything else? Because we've got work to do today. I promise we won't escape to Canada. You got everyone's contact information so just come back when you need us and let me know when I can have my dumpster back," I crossed my arms across my chest. I wasn't mad at Chad but I was still very annoyed at being treated like a suspect.

"When does your other staff get here? We may need a statement from them too. It all depends on trying to figure out the timeline of when the body was dumped," Chad sipped from his paper coffee cup, "And call me when you don't want a sissy boy anymore."

Chad shot Khai a knowing look before heading out to join the officers outside processing the scene. Khai didn't hear what Chad said about him across the busy coffee house but I was fuming angry about it.

Inside my coffee house uniformed officers were taking up full tables. I was ninety-nine percent sure that we were housing the entire police force at that very moment in some way. There was a line at the order counter, a small cluster by the pick-up side, and a number of them outside hovering around our dumpster.

A tabletop gaming group in the back that usually sets up in the book nook was in the reservation room because there were cops in their spot.

I felt dirty and violated in the worst of ways. I wanted to go upstairs and chug the entire bottle of that tequila and pass out on my cold wood floor. Instead, I changed my apron into a fresh one, thoroughly washed my hands, and made two more batches of each cookie because we had sold out again.

Between the chaos and the Lookie-Lous that came in there, I was out of cookies and muffins again. It was so late in the day by this point I wasn't going to replenish the muffins. I did make a small batch of cheesy quiches that sold out after an hour.

Phoebe missed that morning but I wasn't sure if it was because I was in the back or because she saw the big line and decided I was too busy to chat. I pulled out my phone and opened my inbox to see five unread texts from her.

"I know you're packed today. I got my food to go and maybe we can do lunch again."

"You whore! I saw who was coming out of your apartment this morning! I'm not mad, just a little jealous."

"What the fuck is going on over there?"

"Is everyone okay? There are cops all over the place! I saw Lexi running earlier, is she okay?"

"Chad was just in here, fuck that dude. Not actually fuck him, but can we light his hair on fire or something? For someone to have such pretty eyes I didn't catch a whiff of soul behind them. CALL ME BITCH."

I sent her a quick message saying that if I was able to make it over there today I would but for it to be three o'clock in the afternoon and I haven't stopped baking yet, I couldn't make any promises. I made a mental note to make sure that Khai got paid for their time helping today. The quick 'step in' of an hours' worth of work out of the kindness of their soul has quickly developed into an entire day's work in yesterday's clothes and no shower.

From behind me in the street came a shrill scream of a woman's voice followed by clear screams of: "Is it him?! Tell me if it's him! I have to know!"

I turned to look but I already knew it was vampire Ida also known as Caroline. It looked like her mother and a uniformed officer were holding her back as a body bag was being wheeled out to an ambulance.

Since we were in the middle of downtown, they had to block off the road in each direction to get the ambulance and the number of cop cars in the street. In all the noise and the madness, I had completely overlooked there not being any cars driving by.

I saw Phoebe leaned against her building, sucking on her vape stick. Her back was to me but I already knew she was closing early today and going home. I was tempted to go out there and chat with her while we watched the live drama before us but I knew I had to work. I was going to catch Khai and tell them to go home for a few hours and I'd take over. I also needed to kick Lexi out because she has way worked over her hours already and she's been running around since we first opened.

Gregor pushed open the door behind me and clapped his hands to get everyone's attention in the room. I turned just like everyone else to see what was coming next.

"Hello, hello my friends! Gregor has arrived and I'm here to make you some coffee to die for," He paused to giggle, "Too soon? My bad. Anyway, we have trivia tonight starting at five-thirty. That is just in a few short hours. I am here, I am queer and I'm ready to save the day!" Gregor swept in and started bussing tables and cracking up with the customers.

I noticed he even got a table full of cops laughing as he made his rounds. Gregor mainly worked weekends. He works a ten-hour shift on Saturday and then he'd pick up random hours throughout the week to fill in or when someone else requested days off. This past weekend he had been on vacation, though so he had missed all the drama.

I just stood there in a daze while Gregor made it through the dining area before going behind the barista counter and shooed Lexi away from the coffee machines. There were only three people in line and both

Lexi and Khai had been working through all three of their orders at once.

"I'll be back tomorrow. I want all the deets about you and Khai, k? I know what I heard and I'm so front row center. I'm about to see which one of these cops will drive me home since I can't get to my car. Bye-eeeee," Lexi walked out shoving a cream cheese Danish into her mouth as she pushed the door open with her hip. She still looked pissed but at least it wasn't directed at me.

I finally snapped out of my daze and convinced my feet to move. I stood behind the barista counter just as Gregor sniffed the air around Khai and demanded to know who had fornicated with recently.

I raced over to save Khai and myself from an awkward conversion.

"Greggy baby, who called you? Thank you for being here but how did you know to be here?" I asked quickly. Gregor always seemed to know everything that happens in and around New Bern.

"We live in New Bern: population five-hundred chatty white folk, okay? My sister showed me snap chats of her friends doing street dancing around cops and my cousin Faye called me to ask if I had been there when the dude got murdered and dumped in my nerd shop's basement? When did we get a basement? I decided that I wanted to know for myself so I got on my bicycle and peddled my nosey ass here. I guess this loser finally wised up and dumped that trashy girl and we're back to a wholesome staff of horrible but trustworthy panda bears?" Gregor finished up an orders drink as he spoke and we all paused as he delivered the order to the pick-up side of the counter.

"Okay, I only understood about half of that but no we don't have a basement and as far as we know have never experienced death-like things in my precious coffee house. All of the murders happened outside of this establishment. If it was murder, that is. We know nothing," I clarified.

"We know it was Hammond whats-his-face from those fuck happy vamps that come on Thursdays, though, right?" Gregory asked now cleaning up the barista area. It was rightfully wrecked from our insanely busy day.

"How do you know that? You're a marvelous creature. I'd love to study you like a science experiment," Khai picked up a cookie that had been dropped on the floor and launched it into the nearby wastebasket.

"I know all and I'm everywhere. I miss nothing. No matter how far I am away," Gregory always spoke with such high energy it was easy to forget how serious he could be.

"Like you two. You ain't fooling anyone and that's probably why the trashy girl left. Thank you for that, but still. Don't fuck on the clock, this isn't a brothel," Gregory pointed fingers at us and then back at his eyes like he was keeping an eye on us.

"I'm happy about it but this ain't the place," He said reinforcing his point, "I've been in enough businesses with a kitchen to know that the boss is fucking somebody I just don't want to walk in on it. If one of us is getting dick on the clock and getting paid for it we all should. That's my final opinion on the matter," Gregory pulled out two empty jugs of milk from the mini-fridge and said, "I'm replacing these. You two keep your hands off each other until I'm back."

Khai and I instantly broke out into awkward laughter. This place just wasn't the same without Gregor. He was amazing in the kitchen but his personality was meant to be where the people were and we all knew it. You'd never guess that he was so young from the way he looked. His attitude maybe gave you some clues but Gregor was himself and no one could contest that.

We were finally seeing the other side of the rush and Khai managed to leave shortly after Gregor arrived. I helped set up for Trivia and ended up making one last batch of taco-inspired pastries that were only available on Tuesdays after two o'clock.

I have a thing for repetition, it helped me remember. I also tried to make them earlier in the day before and realized that they didn't look so hot in the display case after a certain amount of time. I only made enough for the regulars that I knew would eat them plus a few extra.

As trivia started to wind down Gregor looked at me and told me to go upstairs.

"You look like shit, Boss. Go to bed. I think I can handle this crowd tonight,"

Gregor gave me concerned face. He managed to sound like he was giving me a compliment although he told me I look like shit.

We had picked up a few extra people for trivia but there were empty seats and I didn't have to bake any more for the day. I had managed to do my prep work while I was actively cooking so really it was just dishes. Gregor said he would do my dishes for me. He physically pushed me towards the door so I went.

8

As I walked up the stairs, I realized that I was smelling some type of food from my apartment. I stopped on the step and grabbed my phone to look at the app that held my door code information.

The last number punched in was Khai's special code. I began to relax and finished walking up the stairs. I wasn't sure I could do another night of coitus from the way my body felt. I honestly wanted to drink wine for dinner in the bathtub and then tuck myself into bed until tomorrow.

I opened the door to my apartment and the first room you walk into is the kitchen from the very small wet room that only held a few jackets and there wasn't even room for my washer and dryer.

I had to convert the second bathroom into a laundry room when I first moved in and then cut the living room in half to replace the bathroom and give myself an office space. There was a better flow this way even though it closed off part of the apartment. It was just me, after all.

Khai was plating some type of pasta dish and his phone started beeping right when he realized I was home. He swiped the screen and opened the oven door to retrieve beautifully toasted garlic bread. It didn't look store-bought from the freezer section like I normally buy myself. The pasta was green and I was unsure about it. He added strips of chicken on top of the pasta and a thick wedge of garlic bread to the plate then he sat the plate on my small kitchen table that usually held everything I didn't feel like putting away at the moment.

"I didn't exactly put everything away. I moved the stuff I had no clue where to put on the table in the living room and I bought these placemats earlier. I just wanted everything to look nice," Khai put the extra garlic bread in the middle of the table in a woven basket I've never seen before and there were cloth napkins in the bottom of the basket making me feel like I was at a fancy restaurant. He had bought a table cloth to cover my vintage vinyl round breakfast table and I could smell the pumpkin candle I sometimes lit while I was in the bathtub.

I realized it wasn't my candle but a brand new one that Khai must have bought while he was away from the coffee house. This had to be too good to be true. Tiff was going to burst through the door any moment to say she was pregnant or something. This just couldn't be real life and happening to me.

"It does look very nice." I managed to say.

"I wasn't sure if you liked to shower after work or what so I'm in no rush. I can put this in the warm oven until you get out. I just wanted it to be available if you were hungry. Gregor had just texted me that he had kicked you out so I could get my timing right," Khai sat down across from me and poured us glasses of red wine, "I know this dish traditionally goes with white wine but I've only ever seen you drink red. I put the tequila in the freezer. I figured you were too drained for an actual drink."

"Uhhhh, you're right. The wine is great. Why is my pasta green? This all looks delicious. It's a good shade of green," I shoved garlic bread in my mouth and chewed trying to tell my anxious self-doubt to shut the hell up so I could enjoy someone doing something nice for me.

"It's an avocado pesto. I've made it before and really liked it. I wanted to share it with you. I wasn't sure if you'd like pesto but we've never really eaten pasta together. I know you eat out a lot but I like cooking and I wanted to cook for you."

I just sat there in shock, looking at Khai's face made me want to burst into tears. This had to be the absolute sweetest thing anyone has ever done for me and all I could think about was how the universe was going to ruin it. I just knew something was going to happen and all of this would just be a memory I came back to when the darkness swallows me whole. Instead of talking, I just ate. We ate in near silence.

We made awkward small talk about our day and discussed our favorite seasons. We both agreed that autumn was the best but the cold weather isn't great. We both hate the summers here and Khai was considering moving back to Maine where his sister lives with her girlfriend and five dogs. The move didn't happen because there was this woman that completely captivated them and they had hooked up once after too many drinks at a bar.

Khai's sister had told him that dating their boss was a terrible idea but they knew that they didn't have to rely on the coffee house paycheck for too much longer because the internet business pays all of their bills. Khai had only taken the job at the coffee house to pay for the initial start-up costs of his online gaming business.

Khai knew Tiff from a college when they were taking classes to get certified in software and hardware computer building stuff. I guess he did find her attractive but there wasn't any longevity there from her job aspirations and her personality. Tiff had also discovered romantic feelings that were growing within Khai but those feelings were not geared towards her. Those feelings were geared towards an untouchable person that just couldn't leave their mind no matter how hard they tried.

By the time I got a refill of my wine and my plate was scraped clean my body was relaxed and I felt like I could fall asleep in the chair sitting up at the table. Our conversation went in organic directions and it felt so nice. Is this what being in a relationship is meant to feel like? I tried to recall any moment in my relationship with Lana that felt this comfortable. My brain couldn't recall any good moments and that's when I decided to let all of those bad thoughts leave my brain for at least this evening of being taken care of.

"If it would be okay, I'd like to stay another night with you?" Khai got up from the chair across from me and walked over to me. I dreamily put my wine glass down and stood up too. Khai hugged me and rested their head on my shoulder. We just stood there and hugged. I felt like my heart could explode. It felt so nice to just be held. After a few long moments, Khai slowly pulled back and started cleaning up.

"Of course, you can stay. Don't worry about the dishes. I'll clean them tomorrow." I yawned seriously big, "Just come to bed."

"When will you have a chance to do them tomorrow? It'll take me five minutes to load your dishwasher right now."

"Okay, fine. Clean my house if you want to. I'm going to lay down," As soon as my head hit the pillow, I saw darkness and nothingness until my alarm went off and I instinctively started to roll out of bed until I heard soft snoring.

9

It took me a full minute to remember that I had a sleepover last night with my favorite employee yet again but this time I was still in my pajamas. Nothing had happened in the night and I felt mostly rested this morning. I only had hit the snooze button once before I was out of bed and in the shower. I was able to get ready at my regular pace this time and wore my full-blown attire. More is always better in my opinion. I suffered in the cold on the way down the stairs until I got to the industrial coffee maker and started a batch of drip coffee.

I walked to the ovens while the coffee was brewing and turned them on to preheat. By the time the ovens got hot, I'd have the first pastries ready to go in. Since the day before was so busy I had already spooned out my cookie dough for today and I pulled those sheets out of my walk-in fridge to warm up some before going into the oven. I also decided to switch the Air Conditioner from the front of the house into Heat. I needed that weird burning smell to go away before customers came in, anyway.

I was busy getting the final batch of Baby Muffins done when I heard a knock at the employee door. I sat the hot pan down and walked over to the back door, slowly opening it until I saw Tiff standing there looking like she was about to jump me. I kept the door opened barely a few inches.

"What are you doing here? Didn't you quit?" I asked already bored by what she could possibly say.

"You old bitch, you just couldn't help yourself, could you?" She screamed at me but didn't move forward.

"Look, I don't know what you're talking about. You need to leave. I'll mail your last check. Don't come back here," I started to close the door when she lunged forward and shoved a wad of papers at me. I instinctively jerked back but didn't slam the door when I realized the letters wouldn't hurt me.

"Look at these letters! Khai wrote them to me! Khai loves me not you! You just seem like better bait as an older woman that makes all this money. I'm about to graduate though. Just you wait! Just you wait! I'll get you, ya old bat! Just wait!" The papers hit the ground and went everywhere.

Tiff turned away from me and started stomping away across the back parking lot. I looked over at my car and it looked normal. Most people didn't even realize it was mine, I guess. I've had to stop the building owner from towing it twice because he thought someone was stealing my spot. Nope, that beat-up wagon is mine. It was an ugly beast of a car but it got me where I needed to go if I needed wheels to get me there. I pulled the door shut and bent down to get the papers.

"Well, that's just awkward." Khai was saying before sipping coffee from one of the coffee shop's ceramic mugs.

"How the hell did you get out of my apartment and she not see you?" I asked, flipping through the pages in my hands.

"I guess she went to my apartment yesterday and I never arrived because I got stuck behind the counter here. Then I only went home long enough for a shower and supplies. I bumped into her at the grocery store when I was on my way back. I told her that I wasn't kidding when I said I couldn't see her anymore. She asked me who I was going to cook for and I didn't lie to her. I hope that's okay, she had already guessed. I had just always denied it before. I never expected her to do that. She thinks we had always been together behind her back, I think. We both know that's just not true. If anything, it made me fall for you more because you never seemed petty about her and me," Khai bit into the white chocolate macadamia nut cookie in their other hand and took another sip of coffee.

"You're down here early," I wanted to desperately talk about anything else than Tiff and her being with Khai in any capacity.

"Yeah, Lexi called out," Khai shrugged before sipping more coffee to rinse the cookie down, "She said she had nightmares all night and couldn't get the image of vampire guy in the dumpster out of her head so she's got an appointment with her therapist. We decided it would be better if she sat today out."

"Lexi called you? Why didn't she call me?" What kind of useless boss am I? I pulled my phone from my pocket and saw that I had a few dozen missed texts from people who had heard about the dead guy in the dumpster yesterday and then finally Lexi, she had called me twice and sent me three direct text messages. I need to get better at paying attention to my phone.

"She sent it in the group message. Don't worry Tiff already removed herself. I just said I was close and already awake so I might as well take the shift," Khai licked melted chocolate from their thumb before continuing, "Gregor said he wants to make up for his lost hours so he's filling in for my regular shift this afternoon. We're all happy to not have to work around Tiff anymore. I just heard the yelling and had to make sure you were okay."

"While you sipped your coffee and stole a cookie?" I quipped.

"I'm good for it. You get a pound of flesh later for it. You sleep, okay? I think you barely moved a muscle the entire night." Khai drank a little deeper from the mug.

"Yeah, yeah. I slept like the dead." I paused, "Well, a comfortable well-fed dead person. It was nice to have someone in the bed with me, too. I felt very warm and cozy this morning," I couldn't help but croon a little.

"I hope you don't mind; I borrowed a shirt. The clothes I had brought weren't work clothes," Khai tugged on the Java Tavern shirt that I had cut the neck out of so it was in a jagged V neck. It hung crooked showing off one of their collarbones. The top of the Khai's chest tattoo barely peeked over the neck of the shirt. I was tempted to trace the black ink with my fingers but kept my hands to myself.

We are at the stage of our relationship that I'd prefer Khai to have no clothes on at all if we were being honest. This is a relationship, right? The messy unbalanced steps into the potential of domestic bliss.

"That's okay. I dig you wearing my clothes. Par for the course, I guess. I think that's what that means," I nervously laughed, "I feel way more here today than I was all day yesterday. As long as no one else shows up dead and the cops aren't flooding the place, today may end up to be decent, right?"

Khai smiled and tilted their coffee mug at me like a toast. I pretended to have a mug and we tapped our knuckles together in a toast. It was little moments like this that made me feel so drawn to Khai. Just casual conversation with light flirting. No pressures of guilt thrown at me for existing. It also helped that during work hours I felt like I had the upper hand, the more powerful being, the boss.

I had only had to flex the boss muscle a few times when I first started the coffee house but the team now needed little guidance through their shifts. My employees all show up and get their work done, they police themselves most of the time: Hence the group chat. The group chat was where they all cuss each other out for not refilling the milk fridge or leaving the bathrooms a complete mess.

Lexi typically handles those arguments and I just check on both parties to make sure I wouldn't have to list a job opening soon. I know that working with the public is hard and it is sometimes easy to take it out on your coworkers who put up with the same amount of bullshit from strangers every day.

We all worked out a system that seems to be working so I didn't mess with it much. I honestly didn't realize how bonded everyone was until I hired Tiff. I thought Lexi would be relieved to work slightly fewer hours and be paid the same but after Lexi met Tiff it became something else entirely. No one outwardly told Tiff to go fuck herself, but I felt like Lexi tested Tiff constantly and Tiff consistently failed those tests.

We heard the front door ding and Khai turned without a word to help the customer. I went back to finishing up in the kitchen. With all my prep work the previous day I had given myself an extra hour that I wasn't sure what to do with. I was tempted to do more prep work but until the pantry delivery arrived there wasn't much I could do.

Mondays was a dairy and egg delivery from a local dairy farm and Wednesday was my big corporate restaurant delivery of dried goods. I wanted to source everything locally but my town was just too small and I simply couldn't afford to support a local company in that way. I had tried local companies but they couldn't match the prices close enough for me to turn a profit and have a fourth employee.

The fourth employee was always supposed to be my bakery assistant, not front-of-house staff. Ideally, I'd love to have someone come in around five in the morning when I'm halfway done with my baking, and finish up what I haven't gotten to with me and then do all of my prep work before they finish out their day helping Lexi.

That could just be too good to be true. I'd ask Gregor if he was interested in being my baking assistant anyway, I decided. If was able to finish my regular baking up quicker with an assistant I may be able to sleep in until five in the morning during the not-so-busy season. Those two glorious hours of extra sleep made such a big difference in how I handled the world around me.

I walked back out to the front and most of the tables had customers in them and the front windows were firmly closed this morning. There were only two people in line and they seemed together. Khai was plating a few pastries for them to eat here. I noticed that Khai was making another round of drip coffee and nearly half of the big batch of Baby Muffins were gone. I had made extras of everything today just to be on the safe side. I also had to make more chocolate chip cookie dough and I went ahead and made a full batch of the dough for my mother's thing this weekend. I figured I'd just sell the leftover dough as baked cookies in the Tavern and call it a wash.

The way the week panned out I'd have to bake those cookies Saturday morning anyway so I might as well sell them in-house too. That's when I realized that I could invite Khai to my mother's awkward dinner party. Khai's presence would mortify her and maybe I'd never be asked to go back there when she had guests over again. I'd have to see if that would be something Khai would be comfortable with, though. I have no choices when it comes to being around her but Khai does.

"Hey Khai, I have an awkward as hell question for you," I tried to sound casual. I waited until the customers were halfway to their table before I worked up the nerve to ask.

"You want to marry me already? I already have the dress picked out. Don't you worry," Khai bent down to drag the stack of pre-assembled carry-out boxes to the front of the shelf and shove the next ones behind it and so on. This was how we knew if we needed to make more boxes or not, from the gap.

"Um, close enough to a marriage proposal, I guess. My mom has forced me to come to some rich people's party at her house this Saturday and I was wondering if you'd be my date?" I nervously twisted one of my rings on the opposite hand as I spoke.

"You can say no. I know that I wish I could. It would just be nice to have someone there that's more like me for the night. Honestly, if you say yes, you may hate me after, anyway. This is a selfish risk I'd like to take though if you're willing," I was rambling but Khai was still organizing so I had no idea what was going on in that head of theirs.

Khai stopped organizing and stood up completely facing me.

"Could I dress as me? However I like? Or am I going to have to be male passing and pretend?" Suddenly Khai got weird and still. Khai's voice seemed a little sad and worried.

"No, no, no. Wear whatever you like and be you. I'd never ask you to be something you're not," I shook my head.

"If you are worried about the social anxiety part: I'm asking you there for my emotional support if I'm being honest," I confessed, "Those old fucks are judgy as hell. My mom shows me off at these parties and I always end up at the kids' table if you know what I mean. I'm her one surviving kid and she's trying to work with what she has, I guess. I always present as my true self and drink all the free booze I can get my hands on, then I pass out in my childhood bedroom until the next day and escape when my alarm goes off," I was squeezing my fingers with the opposite hand, trying to read the blank expression across Khai's face.

The phone started ringing and a customer came to the counter for a refill of their drip coffee. I gave free in-house refills on drip coffee because all of the surrounding restaurants did and I wanted people to come here for dessert if they had to make a choice.

"Sure. I'll do it," Khai said once we were customer free again, "You're going to help me get dressed though and I want to see what you're wearing. We will coordinate and explode the minds of those old yuppies, okay? If one old man doesn't get into my face because he's spitting angry it'll be a boring night," Khai patted my shoulder in a comforting way, probably to push it down from my ears because I was so tense.

This was also a new side of Khai I'd never seen before: insecure and willing to outwardly go against the flow. Khai was very vibe-riding although appeared different. Khai never physically made waves around them. Now that I think about it, I've never seen Khai any of the extreme emotions. Always silly but yet serious and filled to the brim with computer facts.

A customer came up for another round of pastries. While my romantic interest was sidetracked, I took a moment to take an inventory of their aesthetic. Khai just wants to exist as their definition of themselves and take every day as it came. Their shaggy jet-black hair barely went down past their eyes, light caramel brown eyes and skin a beautiful cinnamon color. I never asked about their ancestry because I had never really thought about it. Suddenly I wanted to know everything I could about Khai though and what life was like in Maine before moving south. I decided to save that conversation for another day.

For now, I'd just drink them in every opportunity I had. Far back in my subconscious I recognized something about Khai but I was having trouble placing it. I pushed the idea down. That doesn't make any sense and I have too much going on to try and figure it out.

10

We worked through the shift with very little conflict and no dead bodies showed up in the brand-new dumpster we were given by the trash company. The cops had impounded the other one and I was happy about it.

The side door worked in the new one and the paint looked fresh. This dumpster hasn't been backed into a dozen times either so the walls were stiff and unblemished. I wanted to walk around it like one would a brand-new car but it made me feel silly that I got such gratification out of a new dumpster.

"They just dropped it off," I heard Phoebe's voice behind me so I turned around, she was sucking on her vape pen, this one had marijuana in it, "I'm pleased. Our other dumpster was just as much trash as the shit we put inside of it," She laughed.

"Can I have a hit of that?" I walked over to her and she extended the vape pen towards me. She never let go while I took a long drag from it. I exhaled slowly, "Thank you. That was a very needed gift you just gave me," I hoped I'd feel some type of relaxed soon.

"I'm sorry I didn't make it over there this morning, Kayleigh had to quit. She said she was scared if she kept working on this street, she'd end up in the dumpster too. I had to go to work early and do all the shit she didn't finish yesterday and by the time I had finished it was time to open," Phoebe took another long drag and offered me another that I accepted.

"Tiff quit too. I'm not finding a replacement just yet though. I'm going to see if Gregor wants to help me more in the kitchen and then I'll look for someone to take over more weekend hours. It's really just one day to find coverage for, but I'll make him full-time too like Lexi. That way I could balance the front with two part-time workers with Lexi. I think it's time I grew my team, last quarter was way better than I thought it would be," We sat together on the bench in front of her boutique, the pen suddenly disappearing into some hidden pocket in her flowy outfit.

"But doing the whole interview process is such bullshit. I hate spending five days reading hundreds of applications just so the twelve people I interview either decide they don't want the job or they accept a better offer the day before they're supposed to start. That's how I end up with all these high school kids that steal shit from me," Phoebe picked at her nails.

"Post a flyer at The Java Tavern and hold your interviews over there. I'll screen some applications for you too. We'll do this together," I smiled, trying to brighten my friend's day, "I'll see if Lexi knows anyone looking for a job too. She looks normal enough to know other normies, right?" That's when Phoebe finally broke into a smile.

"How is Lexi, anyway? Didn't she find the body?" Phoebe had perked up a bit at the change of subject.

"She called out today so Khai is covering. Gregor is covering Khai's shift. I feel like my whole world is on its side and Barbara wants me to go to a dinner party on Saturday," I rubbed my temples and leaned my head back to let it hang behind me.

"Need a plus one? Maybe I could bag an old dude that will pay all my bills," Phoebe giggled, the vape was working.

"Well, I invited Khai but you could come too. The more the merrier! I've never brought anyone to these things before because they're horrible but you'd blend in with the others there. I'm sure some of the women there have shopped at your store before. There is an old man or three for your choosing. I wish I was joking," I could feel the laughter bubbling within me. I tried to muster up my thickest southern drawl: "My mom would hate the competition of a young thing like you."

"Okay, okay. It's a date. A threesome date. If the night goes bad, I'm going home with you and Khai and we'll be a throuple of love, okay? I'm only kind of joking. I'm about ready to hang an out of order sign on myself and call it a day," Phoebe laughed a full bellied laugh. It took her a moment to recover before I could respond.

"Coupling isn't that important, Pheebs. I just went five years without a relationship and I survived. You can make it a few more months or years if you needed to. Romance is hard, fucking is easy and friendships are where your companions are!" I tried to sound peppy and enthusiastic. I did mean it when I said relationships weren't too important. People focus too much on the prospect of love and forget themselves in the process.

"Yeah, yeah, yeah. Says you that got busy two nights in a row with a sexy younger person that probably predicts all your kinks without you telling them," Phoebe got to her feet and adjusted her dress and cardigan, "I demand free cookies and a hot hibiscus green tea, Madam Coffee Slut."

"Then follow me for all your desires to be met, malady," I did a jester-type bow with my arm extending out towards The Java Tavern.

Phoebe always paid when we went out somewhere and I always gave her free pastries and coffee at my place. This arrangement had organically happened and I somehow still felt like I was taking advantage of her somehow. I even started giving her employees free drinks once we got to know them. In return, her employees always became regular customers and brought paying customers with them on trivia nights and weekends. The ones old enough to drink sometimes came over for a beer after a hard day of retail. The boutique closed at six in the afternoon like most of the other storefront businesses in the entire downtown area.

It was now one o'clock and Khai was still behind the counter. Khai had propped up on the barstool reading a trashy love novel someone had left in the book nook. They gave us a quick glance up but didn't get up from the barstool as we entered from the front door. The way they smiled down at the book once they thought I wasn't looking in their direction anymore just did things to me.

Phoebe and I bussed a table together and cleaned it off before sitting down. There were other available seats but this booth was our regular spot. It was in the far corner of the large extended seating area. I could see behind the barista counter and all of the dining area too. There were a few of my regulars tuning out the world on their laptops clacking away at their keyboards but for the most part, we were alone.

"Tell me how great it is. I just wanna know. Give me the dirty deets, lady. I think you're high enough to be willing to talk," Phoebe asked once we were all settled in with our warm beverages and sweet snacks. She was on her second cookie and sipped carefully from her large mug of tea.

"It's wonderful. Last night we just slept in the same bed after they made me dinner. It doesn't feel real. Tiff quit in a rage this morning and threw love letters at me that Khai supposedly written her. I didn't read them, it felt too personal. Khai didn't even seem phased that I had them. She called me an old bat," I sipped my beer and pushed my quiche around on the plate with my fork.

"You may be batty but we are not old. I refuse to feel old. Not the way society tells us we're supposed to feel old, anyway. I've got a lot of life to live and I don't want to waste any more time. My daughter called me last week to tell me that she's expecting a kid. I'm going to be a fucking grandma. I just don't know how to feel about any of this," Phoebe rubbed her face with both hands and suddenly she looked very tired.

"Gwen is old enough to have babies?" I asked, constantly forgetting that Phoebe had an entire life before I met her.

"Yeah, she's twenty-four. She got married last year to her college romance. His family owns the local newspaper in the small Georgia town where they live. Old money family type deal. Her dad paid for absolutely everything and her new husband's family covered the reception, just like good southern families do," She exhaled slowly, "That was the last big outing I had with Dan before he announced he wanted to marry his girlfriend and we needed to live separate. I half expected him to ask if we could still date while he married this other woman. *Men,*" Phoebe sighed heavily.

"I'm just trying to enjoy the good stuff while it's still good. I know something is going to happen or I'm going to find out some dark thing about Khai that's going to ruin it but I don't want to think about it. I'm just trying to prepare myself so I'm not completely broken when whatever it is crashes down on me," I drank deep from my glass. I could feel the buzzy high feeling start to slip away already.

"You really like Khai, don't you?" Phoebe's eyes widened.

"I can't help it. I know this is the beginning and that's when it's the best but we've known each other since I opened this place. Khai and I have been friends for almost four years now and the sex only happened within the last year," I pushed around the condensation on my beer glass with a finger while I spoke.

"I lied to you before, we had hooked up twice and had kissed a bunch of times after closing down this place," I confessed although Phoebe's expression told me she wasn't that shocked, "I just didn't want to feel like I was grooming Khai to be mine or something. I keep trying to remember who kissed who first but it's got to be me. Khai is so good about asking for consent and well, I'm just not that great at asking first. Luckily it was with good reception or I'd probably have a lawsuit on my hands."

I drank more of my beer because my mouth went dry thinking about how bad my life would have been if Khai wasn't receptive to my forward advances and how lucky I was in the moment.

"Well, I know Khai well enough to know that you wouldn't have gotten to kiss a second time if it wasn't welcomed. Tiff was always picking fights anyway. She was toxic. I could sometimes hear it through the wall. Our registers are attached to the same wall, ya know. I hear the best stuff from your employees sometimes," Phoebe chuckled to herself.

"Really?" I wanted it to be true because that validated a lot of what Khai was saying already. They just weren't a good match together so I shouldn't feel guilty.

"Oh yeah. Tiff totally knew that Khai had a thing for you the entire time. They yelled about it constantly. Every time you'd leave or go to the kitchen, she'd make a jab in Khai's direction about you. I'm surprised some of your regulars never brought it up to you," Phoebe sipped her tea, attempting to hide her smirk.

"Okay, you win. I feel vindicated," We both sat in silence and I let my ears open up to hear the soft jazz music playing over the speakers. We played a mix of high fantasy compositions from nerdy movies and classical jazz that you'd typically hear in a coffee shop. The blend worked well for the demographic.

Wednesday passed through my fingers with barely a hitch. On Wednesday night we have wine pairings with desserts. People could pay a flat rate and get three small wine pours with three half servings of pastries, sweet or savory depending on the wine.

A local winery sent a representative to set up and help sell full bottles of the wine for that night only. It helped move the bottles of wine we had lingering. I only offered three different kinds of wine at any time and the tastings helped me order fan favorites. Around this time of year, I'd carry a fourth seasonal wine that the winery specialized in and had a small display for people to purchase the full bottle on their way out.

The wine seemed to be an easy product to push as last-minute gifts and gifts for hosts during the holiday party season. Otherwise, full bottle sales only happened on Wednesdays or not at all the rest of the year.

Khai stayed for the wine tasting but as a customer. They sat with the Pathfinder group that played together on Friday nights. It looked like they were mapping out their next campaign so I didn't bother them much. I kept catching Gregor staring at me quizzically while we stood behind the barista counter together.

"Can I help you, sir?" I asked in my best boss voice.

"I've never seen you like this before. I like it," He smiled as he spoke. I watched as he made himself a hot tea in the travel mug he left here to hold his beverages of choice.

All employees were required to have a personal reusable cup with a lid to drink out of. I would gift them a travel mug if they didn't have one and they had their shelves in the back for their belongings when they were here and could leave the cups in the cubbies on their time off.

"Like what?" I resisted the urge to pull out my phone and turn the camera so I could see my face.

"I'm not sure if it's love yet but it's something. I approve of this but only because it hasn't affected my paycheck. If anything, it made everything better because I get Thursdays back and my Saturdays just became less annoying," Gregor put the teabag in the hot water and put a shot of lavender and honey into his mug before swirling it in his hand. After he was satisfied that the water had moved enough in the mug he put it down so the tea could steep.

"I'm not sure what it is, Greggy. I just know I'm not overthinking anything. I'm just coasting until I crash. Hey, I wanted to ask you, how would you feel about going full time? I think it's about time I officially made you an assistant baker. Lexi will have to help me find your front-end replacement and I'd have you doing all the baking on Saturdays but come in during the week to help me bake and prep for the next day. I can't keep waking up at three am every day anymore. With you helping me I could sleep until five and that would make me feel closer to a complete human," I looked at him with pleading eyes.

"Well, when you put it like that how can I refuse?" He laughed, "What would my hours be like? I want Tuesdays off still, this week was special and doesn't count."

I went over the details with him and we mapped out a future schedule. This all hinged on Lexi feeling better about coming back to work and her help on hiring someone else, but we hatched a solid schedule idea and already my shoulders were relaxing at the idea of not working every weekend for the rest of my life.

If it all went well by November we would be in a routine and have a new part-timer or two behind the barista counter to handle the holiday traffic. If I was lucky, they'd both stay through the new year but seasonal help around here was even harder to come by than regular staff. Maybe I should hire three people and hope that one of them stays.

I was looking into the dining area when I noticed Barry standing next to a table in the dining area. My spirit guide was standing eerily still behind an older gentleman with a woman next to him I recognized.

I realized I was looking at Lucius in regular clothes and another vampire LARP player that must be his wife, although they both role-played as other people's partners in the kink group. Those other people were sitting across from them also enjoying the wine pairing.

I grabbed a bottle of red wine and told Gregor to ring it up under my account. I cashed myself out at cost at the end of every month just to keep track of things I gave away to people. I uncorked the wine before walking across the dining room table and slid my chair up to the four-top table the couples were sitting at. They looked at me confused as I plopped down in the chair. Barry tipped his hat before dissipating into a thin mist that no one seemed to notice.

"Hi, I'm the owner of this establishment and sometimes I like to give people free drinks and get to know them better. Look at this bottle as a bribe for information," I topped off everyone's small glasses that held that same wine in them, "Everyone enjoying their evening?"

"Excuse me, this is very kind of you but we'd like to continue our private conversation here," Lucius of course took the lead in the conversation.

"Hey, if you're doing drugs in my place of business and dumping bodies in my dumpster, I have the right to have some small talk, right?" I was feeling bold. I noticed Khai giving me worried glances from across the dining area. I was speaking in hushed tones but Lucius wasn't being very quiet.

"I have no idea what you're talking about," Lucius reached up and nervously loosened his tie. The couple across from them both drank from their newly refilled wine glasses without a word.

"Oh, get over yourself, Talbot. She's made us. Our costumes only get us so far, you know. That's why I wanted to keep it in the basement," The woman beside him, I'm assuming Lilith, spoke, "I feel so sorry for poor Ham. That was a decent kid. It feels like such a waste that he's gone."

Tears spilled over onto her cheeks and she discretely tried to dab them away with a paper napkin. The tears seemed genuine but she didn't want to make a big fuss about it.

"We liked Hammond, he went to all of our parties, even before we got into the Vampire thing. We were all very close," The man spoke from across the table, giving Lilith some time to regain her composure. "We love your place. The Java Tavern is our main hangout. I grab coffee and pastries from here every morning on my way to work."

"We've all agreed to move on from all of this and tomorrow we are hoping to host an in-character funeral for Thorny at our usual time and just move on from there. I was going to pay for it on my way out tonight. The spot is still open, right?" Lucius was very curt and a smidge too loud but it wasn't much different from any other interaction I'd had with him.

"Give the girl a break, Talbot. The cops have been up her ass too. We both read that article in the paper. It's not her fault. She's not the one that—" Lilith choked back her tears, "That murdered our friend. She's just as annoyed at the inconvenience of that boy's death as you are. At least you get to be annoyed while poor Ham will never be annoyed by anything else for the rest of time."

Lilith abruptly got up from her chair and rushed into the bathroom and shut the door behind her.

"I'll go check on her," The other woman got up and went to the bathroom, after a soft knock on the door, Lilith let her disappear behind the door too.

"See, you upset her. Good job," Talbot slash Lucius drank his wine like a shot at a frat party.

I pushed the wine bottle to the center of the table and got to my feet.

"The table is still available for tomorrow. I won't accept payment because of what it's for. I'll arrange for everything just like usual but I'll cover the cost in Ham's honor. This wine is on the house too. Have a great rest of your evening," I replaced my chair from the table I had stolen it from and walked back across the coffee house.

"Well, I think I'm done for the day," I told Gregor once I got back to the counter. "I'm going to run the dishwasher before I go up to give you a jump on closing. I'll bus all the tables before I do, though."

"Thanks, Boss," Gregor said as he sipped his tea.

The wine rep had already packed up all of her stuff and returned the box of wine she wasn't able to push, along with all the money from the wine bottles. After I ran the first load of dishes there wasn't much for Gregor to do to close everything down for the night.

Khai was still in the middle of an in-depth six-way conversation when I was heading out so I didn't want to disturb them. I sent a text to Khai about going upstairs after their meeting and let them know I was just sneaking out so I wouldn't disturb their planning session.

11

I punched in the code to gain access to my stairwell and as soon as I opened the door Barry was standing in the middle of the hallway with his arms crossed over his chest. He didn't have to say anything because I could sense his mood.

"Hi, Barry," I said with a smile as I walked through his wispy form.

"That's completely rude of you and I won't stand for it," Barry insisted, "Especially after I assisted you with information regarding that poor trash receptacle fellow," He hovered directly over my shoulder as I made my way up the stairs and into the apartment.

"You can't stand for anything anymore, remember?" I was not in the mood for this tit-for-tat that Barry insisted on, "You told me about that information in a way that got you pretty flowers for your grave."

"And that, my dear, is called a win, win situation. I have kept my distance because you've had a gentleman caller and

I'd rather not be a part of your flesh games so I must keep this brief before your man arrives once more," Barry straightened up and rested his arm on his astral cane.

My spirit guide wore very formal clothes and the cane was from some type of war wound that would later contribute to his death after he caught influenza brought over from an English ship in the late seventeen hundredths. He always complained that he still needed the cane even though the pain didn't hurt anymore, it only lingered in memory.

"Khai doesn't like those pronouns," I couldn't resist correcting Barry at any chance.

Barry would never change some of the backward thinking that was completely normal in his day but he made strides in other ways, like not calling me a whore for the premarital coitus I enjoyed as much as I could manage.

"Anyway, as I was saying," Barry said without much hesitation, "I have information on the trash receptacle fellow, he should be out there wandering around. I've tried to help him reach out to you because you're the one that can speak to him but he's rather shell-shocked, I'm afraid. Dying that way can do it to you. He's tied to the water fountain across from the church. Something about the flowing water has him fully captivated. He has sat on that bench staring at that water since his soul manifested early Sunday morning. The poor man is completely unresponsive."

"So, he did die Saturday night?" I asked, figuring out the timeline.

"Maybe. One does not know when the soul manifests as a spiritual form. There is no consistent time to use as a reference. I once met a lovely gal from the nineteen twenties. She had come here to marry a rich business owner only to slip in the water closet and poor thing died from a head wound to the stone tub. She didn't manifest until late last year when someone bought the home she died in and ripped out that death-dealing bathtub. It's all rather strange, really," Barry amused himself by his story of woe and cleared his throat, "Now you run on ahead and speak to him and I'll keep an eye out for your bedfellow. I'll ring twice for skedaddle."

I groaned, I did not want to go up and down my stairs again. I poured myself a beer from my fridge in a travel coffee mug. Quickly I made the journey down the stairs to cross over the back parking lot to the alley that had the water fountain in it.

The round, triple-layered fountain was embellished and ornate. A crane perched at the top with its beak facing skyward. This was not a public drinking fountain but a water feature that trapped more lost souls than I liked to acknowledge.

Most of the time I avoided this alleyway. The running water near a religious structure is meant to confuse harmful spirits and I did not need evil entities attaching themselves to me. My bad luck was bad enough, thank you very much.

The beer helped me communicate with one individual spirit. Beer was created to help live humans thriving in a time that death was prevalent just by drinking unclean water. The wheat and barley purified the water to make hydration safer and therefore launched civilization into safety in the shape of structured villages and towns.

We owe beer our very existence and the witches that brewed it for generations always included protection spells to those who consumed the concoction with respect.

My beer was canned craft beer from a local brewery that had female brewers on staff. These types of connections made the brew more mystical for how I was using it. I always made sure to bless these beers before I put them in the fridge and kept crystals on the tops of the cans in the fridge so I knew not to just drink them just for funsies.

I sipped the beer and clutched the crystal necklace I always wore for protection. Souls that experienced violent deaths weren't the most pleasant towards the living. We all looked like their murderers or the causation of their untimely demise. They had what I call a bad death.

Barry had a good death even though he died of sickness, so he was able to come back and be productive to the living. Barry had managed to father a few sons; pass on a family fortune and was on his third wife by the time he passed. Even by today's standards, he had led a full life. Hammond on the other hand, had his life ripped out from under him and then had his flesh suit dumped in the literal trash. This could go very bad... very, very bad. I drank a deeper sip of the beer and pushed the crystal deeper into my palm. I had a quickened my step because I didn't want to explain my sudden absence to Khai if I didn't have to.

I could see the shadow of what had to be Hammond as my feet touched the brick alleyway. The fountain worked on regular spirits too, not just angry or evil ones. I tried to build a spectral wall around Hammond on the bench. This would block out any interference once I started to communicate. I wish I had grabbed my emergency spell casting kit but this was all in such a rush.

As I got closer Hammond became less of a shadow and more of a flickering image of the kid I had seen in the security footage. He was wearing the same cargo pants and dark-colored bowling shirt that had graffiti-style art across it. The art was so involved it took a minute for your eyes to adjust on the images within all the swirls. I finally saw the image of a face of some space odyssey adventure character in it and other symbols I assumed correlated with the movies. My favorite type of nerd stuff involved other worlds, not space travel, so I only vaguely knew about that stuff.

"Ham," I gently tried to mentally reach out to him without startling him. "Hammond? Thorny?"

Once I said his fictitious name was said his head quickly and unnaturally jerked in my direction. That's when I saw the knife hilt sticking from his face. I tried not to react but I instantly felt the despair and sadness from his spirit.

"I know this is all new to you. Bartholomew sent me. He's my friend. The rumors are true, I can see things that others can't," I paused just to see if I could sense if Hammond was able to follow me, "I know it's hard to communicate right now but I just want to help you get some rest, okay? Bartholomew will help you through the process if you allow it. I want to help avenge you if you know anything I could bring to the police."

I watched as Hammond flicker once and then twice. His image slowly started to fade out and I had no idea if anything I said

144

actually got to him. I popped the lid off of my travel mug and chugged the rest of the beer.

I pulled a single dried sage leaf from my pocket, lit it, and thanked the spirit world for protecting me, and carefully placed the leaf under the bench where it could naturally burn out and no one would bother it, nor would it catch anything else on fire. I pulled a glass marble and some coins from my pocket and buried them in the flower bed behind the bench. These little gifts help me leave haunted areas without attachments.

I had made it upstairs and in the shower before my phone buzzed that someone had gained access to my outer door. Just as I got out of the shower and wrapped a towel around myself, I heard Khai in the kitchen calling out to me so I wouldn't be frightened to hear movement in the apartment.

I used my hand to wipe away some of the fog from the mirror glass. I saw Hammond standing behind me. His unnatural purpleish blue mouth was wide open but no noise was coming through. He still had the weapon stuck in his face but this time I saw him in full color.

A thick stream of blood was oozing down his eye socket. I held my breath trying not to scream. I've seen worse in horror movies, right? Gorey zombie films and the like were nothing compared to this, though. The real-life horrors presented to me as echoes of the past were worse than any movie. These ghastly experiences always made me feel emotionally drained afterward as I felt the emotions of the person showing me their pain.

I gripped the sink with both hands and tried to keep eye contact for as long as possible. I had to hold the connection if Hammond was going to tell me anything. I could feel the knife being entered into my skull right above my eye.

Flashes were sent in my mind. I felt the scuffle of hands flying and I knew that he was fighting for his life. I tried my best to force air in and out of my nostrils so I wouldn't pass out. Before being stabbed in the face Ham had been stabbed in the stomach at least twice. Death wasn't happening fast enough for the angry murderer who seemed to swallow me whole.

Two more flashes: a cufflink, I think? A dress of flowy material that belonged to a blonde-haired person. Bright lights and laughter. A clink of glasses and a flash of vampire teeth.

A soft knock on the door broke the connection and Hammond was no longer behind me in the reflection of the mirror. I was able to breathe normally and I realized I broke a nail from gripping the sink so hard. I clipped the nail off and called to Khai that I'd be out in a moment.

I needed a minute to process what just happened. I could still feel the pain of the blade being pressed into my eye socket.

12

The next morning, I stood behind the barista counter with Lexi post rush to discuss the Gregor idea. She was all about the idea of Gregor becoming a cross-trained employee that could help with the morning shuffle.

She completely trusted his barista abilities, even more than me or Khai. She agreed that it would be easier to get a newly trained person into the evening hours. The evenings were much slower on an average day.

"Oh, and the reservation room is going to have the vampire LARP group tonight, they're doing an in-character funeral for Thorny," I casually worked into the conversation.

"That's going to be weird. What if one of them is the killer?" Lexi's eyes grew huge, "What if I'm a target now because I found the body?"

"You'll be long gone before they get here, don't worry about it. I'm staying to arrange the table and it's Gregor's night to work. He gets here around 2 o'clock. You can leave any time after eleven if you want to. I know answering the same question all morning has started to get to you," I pulled some empty pastry trays out of the display window and stacked them up to bring to the back as I spoke.

"No, I'll stay until two so you can disappear with Phoebe. I worry about that woman," Lexi had real concern on her face, "She's depressed, Eliza. Like, seriously depressed. I went over to her shop yesterday right before she closed and she was crying behind the counter. I guess she hadn't seen a customer in a while and she got lost in her own thoughts. I had startled her. We ended up going back to her place for drinks after she closed up shop."

"Oh?" I tried not to sound too curious. None of this was really my direct business, "How was that? Pheebs mellow out after a drink?"

"Well, to be honest, she hit on me," Lexi paused and took a long drink from her travel mug that had her initials across the side in big curvy letters, "I've never had a woman hit on me before. Especially someone that wasn't after a free coffee. I don't know, we made out some then I went home. I thought it was going to be awkward when she came in here today but it really wasn't. She didn't mention it to you?"

"Don't repeat any of this if she hasn't mentioned it, okay? I don't want to tell anyone's secrets," Lexi suddenly felt a little on edge about telling me, like she was telling me a personal secret that wasn't meant to be told.

"No problem there. Wow. I had no idea. I mean, I had an idea. Phoebe has been making some passes at me lately but I thought it was out of desperation not actually implicating anything. She never pegged me as someone that would stray out of the hetero-lifestyle. You either if we're being honest." I laughed.

"Hey! Sexuality isn't just one cut-and-dry thing, okay? When I agreed to go out with her it was because I know she's your friend and she's going through something. Sometime during the evening, we just sat closer on the couch or something, I don't know. It just happened. If she's not going to make a big thing out of it I won't either. She's only texted me a few times today, which has been a better experience than the guys I've gone to second base with on a first date with. I figured if she hasn't said anything yet she'd ask you to lunch and tell you then. She hasn't said much other than she doesn't regret anything and that she'd love to see me again. Just checking in type stuff. I think she likes that I haven't really done much with a woman too. Losing our virginity together type thing, or something," Lexi tucked a long blonde strain of hair behind her ear and tapped the edge of her mug with her fingers like she had other things to say but was holding back.

"Well, I love Pheebs and I know you both well enough. To be honest I think both of you would work well together for your personality types. I have no comment on the sexual stuff because I've never romanced either of you, but I'm here for the love connection! I support this venture with open arms. Just please don't fuck anywhere people eat or where food goes in here," I brushed coffee grounds off of the table with my hand onto the tile floor.

151

"I'll let you and Khai keep the record on that, thanks," Lexi said before erupting in a full fit of laughter.

"Do I have any secrets in this place?!" I asked, completely dumbfounded.

"Khai doesn't kiss and tell but Gregor knows all. I'm telling you. I'm not sure if someone walked in on you guys or what, but we've all known this entire time that you two hooked up in the kitchen after closing at least once. I'm not even sure who told me or if they even worked here at the time," Lexi went over to the espresso machine and wiped up some grains that had been dropped along the edge of the counter.

"Well shit. Here I thought we were being professional and keeping a lid on it. How did people know?" I grabbed my own travel mug and took a long sip from it.

"Well, from what I was told, there were butt prints on the walk-in fridge door and someone heard you both from outside," Lexi's face flushed a deep red color and my ears were starting to get warm with embarrassment, "I don't see Khai that way but apparently they know what they're doing for you to get that loud."

I covered my mouth just in time to spit my coffee in it. Lexi lost her mind laughing and I excused myself to go clean up in the back. I simultaneously started laughing as tears formed in my eyes.

It took me a full twenty minutes to recover in the back before I came back out to the front. I walked in on Phoebe leaning across the table to gently kiss Lexi on the mouth. My one regular that sat by the window on his laptop in the dining area was completely involved in whatever he was writing, completely unaware of the women kissing behind him.

I loudly cleared my throat and Phoebe's face turned blood red as she leaned away from Lexi, who was suddenly very thirsty, and moved quickly to her travel mug to hide her own blushing face. I didn't even need to fake surprise because I really was shocked that Phoebe or Lexi could be romantically involved with each other.

"I don't know if I could handle any more surprises this week," I mumbled to myself.

"Lunch? Your treat. Let's go for Indian today," I hooked arms with her and it made her twirl around to face the front door, Phoebe blew an air kiss to Lexi on her way out. I tried to not laugh hysterically at the week I was having.

We sat at the Indian restaurant that was a few doors closer to our businesses on Middle Street than the Italian place we had margaritas at on Monday. The Indian Eatery served family-style so we picked an entrée to share and chowed down on the naan bread and hummus they sat at the table before even taking your order. After we had consumed all of the bread on the table, I finally broke the silence.

"Lexi, huh?" I took a long drink of my lemonade.

"I'm not even sure how it happened. I broke down with full-on sobs feeling sorry about myself yesterday in the store. I was mid-cries trying to get the energy to get to the door and lock up early when she came in.

She instantly came behind the counter and hugged me. She pulled out one of those little packs of tissues from her purse and got me to calm down. I offered to buy her dinner or drinks and from how much of a mess I was we somehow just ended up at my house drinking wine and eating delivery," Phoebe paused to sip from her soda.

"I do just live just down the street so she followed me in her car directly from the boutique. After we had a glass or two, I realized our knees were touching and I reached my hand down to pat her thigh. I'm not sure what made me do it but I just rested my hand there and well, before the next glass was poured, she was in my lap kissing me," Phoebe blinked a few times to process the words she was saying.

"It was the hottest make-out session I think I've ever had in my entire adult life. It was something that was unleashed in both of us." Phoebe paused her story while the waiter delivered the food to the center of the table and put empty plates in front of us.

"After what felt like hours we finally came up for air and I wanted her to stay the night but she said she had to let her dog out

155

before he pooped all over her apartment. She's coming over, with her dog, Friday night. I think her mentioning her dog means she's going to stay the night, right?" Phoebe was using the serving spoon to scoop some of the curry and rice onto her empty plate. I loved seeing how animated she was after the weepy couple of weeks she's had.

"I honestly have never caught a gay vibe from Lexi but then again, I struggle to see her as a human person sometimes. She reminds me so much of an angry poltergeist," I laughed, "to be fair, I think she sees me as an extension of the Tavern like I don't exist in reality beyond the threshold of the building. Kind of like how we saw teachers in school growing up."

"Something like that," Phoebe laughed, "She likes you though, as her boss. She said she's never had such freedoms as an employee somewhere before. You let her be her but still stay on-brand for your company. She looks up to you a little, I think. Lexi wants to be part owner, eventually. She has daydreamed about it, anyway. She's closer to your age than mine but she knows coffee is something she's good at and she enjoys it. Lexi also said she'd help me find a new employee for my store. She had the same suggestions, too. She is helping me make flyers to hang up a few places in town when she comes over tomorrow. I bought a printer this morning and it's in my car already."

"I'm happy for you both. I just need to process it all. Monday during lunch you'd think we were going to become Golden Girls together and now it's Thursday and we actually have love lives to speak of!" I wanted to clap my hands and celebrate but instead of shoved curry into my mouth and more naan bread that was brought over in the middle of Phoebe's story time.

Towards the end of the meal the owner came over and made small talk with us, we all knew each other and networked constantly. In our small-town networking and metaphorically rubbing elbows was the only way to stay above water.

We all have helped each other out in some way or another. I actually got my chai recipe from Deepa, the restaurant's owner. Anytime anyone orders a Chai tea my employees and I have all conditioned ourselves to plug her restaurant and give her credit for how delicious the tea is.

I even used the same sources to get the herbs and we shared the ingredients when one of us was running low. We supported each other in that way, even though she thinks my Pumpkin Chai Latte is an abomination, we remain friends.

"I see business has picked up now that you're the murder coffee house," Deepa quipped. I tried to play it off but she persisted, "Did he really get murdered in your kitchens? That didn't seem like real information to me. I heard basement but I know that building doesn't have a basement."

"I don't know where his life was ended. I just know it wasn't inside my building. Not the parts of the building I pay rent for anyway," I tried to not hype up the situation more than it already was.

"You know, I've seen him before. He comes in here sometimes with a few different women. He was quite the ladies' man. I know a few young men seem to pick the Eatery as their first date place but these women came with him on several occasions. They all seemed very romantically interested in him too. I wish my son had that type of draw, maybe he wouldn't spend every weekend in front of his computer if he had someone, right?" Deepa shrugged.

"These women, was one closer to his age and the other one much older? The younger one works at the florist shop across from my place if you've ever seen her in there. The older one has darker hair?" If Lilith was actually going on individual dates with her swinging buddy, I'm sure that was breaking some type of rule and gave her husband lots of motive.

"Yes, that's them! You are like a magician. How do you always know things before I do?" Deepa laughed and we all joined in her laughter to share in the joke.

"I actually didn't know that he ate here a lot, not that I blame him. The food is always amazing here, Deepa. Thank you so much for the awesome meal," the only downside to eating at Deepa's Indian Eatery was that I needed to be rolled out of there every time. I was so full it hurt, "I may need an afternoon nap now."

Phoebe paid the owner directly since she was already at our table and we went back in the direction of our respective businesses.

"Don't tell Lexi all the details I said. I mean, I'm sure she knows I tell you all the details of my life already but I don't want it to be weird between you two. I know you can separate my version of Lexi and the Lexi that runs your coffee business. I just don't want it to be weird between all of us," Phoebe scrunched her face, "Honestly, I'm more worried about it working out and I'll have to explain to my daughter that I'm dating someone only a couple of years older than her... and a woman." Phoebe laughed loudly again but this time we were outside and less people cared about our loudness.

"That will be an interesting conversation, to say the least," Phoebe went on, "For now, I'm enjoying my not-so-secret romance and if someone else can get me off then I think the whole world can relax once more."

I clutched my crystal and over-enthusiastically prayed loudly.

"Dear gods and goddess above and below: please bless this lesbian love to be prosperous and may their love grow and grow for ever more, ahh-man."

Phoebe elbowed me hard in the ribs.

"Ow! I'm only joking. You don't end a prayer to the goddess with amen, that's sanctimonious at best," I rubbed my ribs all the same, though. Her elbow hurt.

We made it back to our part of Middle Street and I saw Lexi sitting on the bench outside of the Boutique. Phoebe broke off with me without a word and sat down beside Lexi. Casually Phoebe stretched her arm out behind Lexi and started gently rubbing the back of her neck. I rolled my eyes; they'd end up in the fitting room of Phoebe's boutique if they kept that up.

I pushed open the door of The Tavern and Gregor was behind the barista counter serving a group of tabletop gamers that had just arrived.

Their Dungeon Master was already setting up at one of the longer tables out in the open and he had names laid out where everyone was going to sit and their character sheets and some notepaper already in their places. I was so tempted to see if I could squeeze my way into their game but I thought about the new information I had and I needed to figure out a way to reach out to Chad in a way that didn't upset Khai or ruin my day.

I had to know if the police had any leads on the murder case. I walked around to check all the tables and get a few cups that had been left on tables before heading back to the kitchen to start making funeral foods.

I've actually hosted a few character funerals in my time as a tabletop coffee shop owner and they've never disappointed me. This would be the first time I hosted one for an actual dead person, though. Usually, about halfway through their role play, they'd switch gears to an exciting "new" character that is joining their group for the very first time.

After refilling a napkin holder, a man in a baseball cap and fleece jacket caught my attention. He was sitting in the booth Phoebe and I usually sat at. He was hunched over a newspaper and kept whispering into his wrist. Clearly a cop. As I approached him, I realized it was Chad and I rolled my head around on my shoulders being extra dramatic. Well, that solved my problem of how to reach out to him after all.

"What are you doing, Chad?" I said in a deadpan voice.

"Shhh, don't out me. I'm here on assignment." He hissed at me.

"Copper man Chad is here. Chad is in the corner, everyone!" I said it loud enough for everyone to hear, the dungeon master and the group of players didn't even glance in our direction, though.

"See, nobody cares. Tiffany Sawyer is in that group. She graduated with us and I already saw her wave to you earlier. We all know you're a cop, dude," I sat down in front of him, still holding half a sleeve of napkins.

"I heard that the vampire group was still meeting here today so I'm here just to see what gets said and if we can use any of that information," He pulled his hat down lower over his eyes and sighed, "I knew I should've worn sunglasses but I thought that would have made me more conspicuous."

"At five in the afternoon in the early fall when it's crazy dark by six? Nah, no one would notice you at all," I sucked my teeth to add to my sarcasm and he was not amused, "Did Gregor tell you about the vampires or did you have a spy at the wine tasting last night?"

"Um, the second one? Not a spy, really. A coworker's wife always has girl's night at your wine tastings and they know you from your tarot readings during Art Walk. They saw you walk over to a table and heard everything. All the wives in the group have cop husbands so they've been following the news reports and probably squeezing their husbands for any details they could get from them about the dumpster case," He pulled the hat off to push down his thick blonde hair and then put the hat back on like it helped him blend in with the non-existent crowd in here.

"So you know that Hammond was banging Lilith, right? Talbot Chandler's wife?" I couldn't help myself but I knew I had to hook him to tell me more.

"Well, that *is* the rumor," He begrudgingly agreed.

"They do E and swap around mates at these things. Not here, but they got to Talbot and Lilith's house to pass each other around or umm, do group things," I added and instantly he was interested again.

"E as in... ecstasy?" He spoke into his wrist.

"Yes," I reached across the table and held his wrist up to my lips, "As in the drug popular for sex parties," I yelled into the small microphone clipped inside his jacket. He instantly flinched from something being yelled into an earpiece I couldn't see and I laughed.

"Deepa from Indian Eatery has spotted Lilith or whatever her real name is at her place with Thorny on actual dates. They don't do that here, it's all fake and fantasy here, but going out to eat in regular normie clothes probably puts a motive on Talbot, right?" I crunched the paper bag of napkins in my lap, "Jealousy or something?"

"You've been watching too many detectives shows from the nineties." Chad blinked at me.

"It's always the spouse," I chided.

"Not always, sometimes it's a family member," He said in a small voice, "Look, I'm not going to argue about this with you. I—" And that's when we saw them arrive, this time they were thirty minutes early so the sun was dramatically descending the far horizon as they entered.

I could see Khai behind them patiently waiting to get inside. I started to get up from the table when Chad dramatically pulled me into his lap and forced a kiss on me. I was kicking my legs and moving my arms but he was strong and I wasn't able to escape.

His lips landed somewhere either on my chin or my neck but with his hat on it was hard to tell from a third party perspective. I instantly sprang from his lap and hit him, knuckles first, across the face as hard as I could. Khai was already in front of us by the time I had gathered myself and was straightening out my clothes.

"That's assault, you piece of shit!" Khai was fuming, their entire face was red; veins were popping out of their forehead and neck. I had never seen Khai past mildly annoyed before. I pushed at Khai's chest and said that we'd just go upstairs until everyone cooled off.

Gregor was very nosey about the whole sitting with Chad situation. While he was eavesdropping on us, he put the teas and small sandwiches I had made earlier in the day, on the reserved table for the vampire LARP group.

I was glad for Gregor not keeping his nose in his own business this time because I was too sidetracked to serve the vampire group. The vampires were all seated by the time I was pushing Khai out the door and Gregor held up four fingers, letting me know that Caroline was not in the group any longer. I had missed their entrance because I was fighting Chad off of me.

13

"I'm sorry, I'm sorry." Khai was bouncing both legs and tears were running down their face as they tried some deep breathing, "I just... I walked in and I saw you getting up. At first, I was annoyed because you were sitting with that straight jacket and then when he grabbed you. I about knocked over one of those vampires to get to you but it was already too late and he had you. He was pressing himself against you. I just lost it. It's going to take me a few minutes to calm down. I'm just glad you were able to handle yourself. You are okay, right?"

I walked over to the freezer and pulled out the tequila and grabbed a lime from my fruit bowl. Instead of a cutting board I just grabbed a plate that looked suspiciously similar to the ones I have downstairs and cut the lime into wedges. I shook the salt shaker over the limes and pulled a couple shot glasses out of the cabinet. They were the big ones that held a double shot, who knows where my single shot glasses went. I poured two shots and licked the skin of my hand right above my first knuckle. I added salt to the damp skin and took both shots before I ate a lime and repoured both shots.

"I'll be okay. Eventually," I said numbly knowing it sounded like an absolute lie.

"Your punch was impressive," Khai said, now joining me in the kitchen, "Remind me to never touch you without consent."

"Do I really need to write it in a memo?" I motioned towards the shots and Khai salted the skin above the knuckle on my hand and right before bending down to lick the salt off my hand Khai's eyes met mine, "Go ahead," I whispered, trying to remember I was upset.

Khai licked the salt from my hand, still held on to my hand while downing both shots and I had put a lime in my teeth with the skin part towards me. Khai used my hand to pull me completely into their frame as their mouth was on mine fighting with my tongue and the lime.

I think we drank half the bottle before passing out in my bedroom. I felt a hand

169

push against my shoulder and my eyes popped open.

We were both naked and twisted up in each other again but Khai was star fished across the bed while I was half hanging off the edge on my side. I had all the blankets and Khai had the whole bed.

I felt the push again and turned my face to see Hammond, sitting on my floor with his mouth open again in a silent scream. Barry was the one pushing on me. There is something about being asleep that allows a physical connection between our reality and theirs. As you're falling asleep or in the process of waking up ghosts are able to touch you in a way that feels physical. Prankster ghosts tug at toes or yank blankets. Barry only utilized this thin veil of opportunity during dire emergencies.

My eyes adjusted to the darkness and I saw the features of Barry's face in the darkness.

"Go. You're in danger. Go!" Barry waved his cane at me to get his point across.

I heard the scraping noise coming from the living room. It didn't feel like a ghost noise, it sounded like a human intruder noise. I glanced at my watch and it was barely past midnight. We had gone to bed closer to my regular bed time: as early as possible.

My head felt a little wish-washy from the booze but I tried to keep myself focused. I stood up and realized my feet were right where Hammond's astral legs were.

"Sorry, sorry," I apologized quickly as I put on pants and a nearby shirt that was thrown over a nearby chair. I shook Khai's leg and tried to wake them up. The snoring was interrupted but Khai remained asleep.

There was an emergency fire exit where the noise came from but you could only access it from the street if you had a lift or ladder. The available ladder extended from the top if you were escaping from the window it was intended for. I kept a few of my plants out there during the warmer months.

I could see a hooded shadow through the window from the street lights. The window the figure was trying to break into was positioned in the living room beside the television set.

"Go, woman! Get your bed fellow and get out of here!" Barry was screaming at the top of his ghost lungs, making it hard for me to focus.

"Will you shut up?" I hissed into the darkness. I tried to crouch down in the kitchen, grabbing the half full tequila bottle as a weapon.

I heard Khai start to wake up in the bedroom behind me. I looked around and after a long moment I watched in horror as the glass was removed from the lower window frame in the living room and without a noise was placed on the emergency exit floor. While the intruders head was turned away, I quickly scampered over to the window and lifted the bottle above my head waiting for the cloaked person to let themselves into my apartment.

"This is an utterly bad idea, young lady! I told you to get out of here and I meant it!" Barry was still screaming at me and Hammond was now standing directly behind him. Ham's face still twisted in a quiet scream and the hilt of an ornate knife stuck out of his eye socket. Ham's good eye shined silver in the darkness of the room.

I watched as the intruder carefully put two feet down into my apartment and then stood up, facing away from me. They stood slightly shorter than my five feet nine inches and I remembered something from my self-defense class. I brought the tequila bottle down on the inside of their knee and they screamed out in pain, waking Khai instantly.

"Eliza? Is that you? Where are you?" Khai was calling out from the bedroom as I brought down another blow to the edge of the hooded person again. The tequila bottle landed right above where their ear was assumed to be. Have you ever been hit in the ear? That shit hurts.

Without more than a few grunts and loud yelp of pain the person climbed right back out of the window and was down the fire escape before Khai was in the living room with me. My 'bed fellow' was wearing only my thick fluffy robe to cover themself. I liked to wear it around the house right after I got out of a bath when I wasn't ready for clothes yet.

I still held the tequila as a weapon and Khai already had their phone to their ear calling nine-one-one to report the break in. I just sat in the floor where I was standing and waited for the cops to show up.

We sat on the floor together holding hands. Khai did put on pants before the cops arrived. I explained that I had heard a noise that woke me. I had trouble getting back to sleep so I had gotten up to investigate and that's when I saw the shadow of a person in the window so I decided to grab the tequila as a weapon. Luckily my defense technique worked and I was happy I didn't have to wait on the cops alone.

"That's a great story to tell the cops but how did you really wake up?" Khai looked at me as if he already knew the answer.

"Barry woke me up," I mumbled.

"Barry as in a not real person, Barry? Or Barry as in you have a roommate I don't know about Barry?" Khai asked with sincerity. I could hear the police sirens in the background, I glanced at my watch, it was now almost one in the morning. My alarm would go off soon.

"Barry is a real person but not an alive person, if that's what you're trying to say. He's a ghost, he's... my ghost. He's my guide from the other side. He chose me and I guess I chose him too. Without Barry I wouldn't have moved back to New Bern, to be honest. He's more family and friend than my actual family and the only friend I had for a long time," I heard the apartment buzzer before Khai could respond and I used my app to grant the police access. Khai got up from the floor to let them in. I got to my feet.

Chad was in plain clothes with the officers and I worried that Khai would finish what was started earlier but the black eye only made Khai chuckle.

"Hey bud, you fall on a door knob or something?" Khai joked. Chad just pushed pass like he hadn't heard anything.

"Are you okay, babe?" Chad was cooing over me.

"Please leave now," I said in a stern voice, "Or I'll tell everyone in here how you got that black eye," I hissed.

"Okay, fine. Sorry I cared about you being in danger!" Chad snapped, turning on his heels and leaving my apartment.

The apartment over the coffee shop is a decently large space but with all of these cops in here and a team from Raleigh, who I assumed was here still processing the dumpster, made my apartment suddenly very small.

My phone started vibrating and my building owner's name appeared across the screen. I answered the call and Mister Billy Bradford's booming voice filled my ear.

"Hi dear, I got a phone call from Charlie's boys telling me someone broke in to the apartment. Are you okay? Was anything broken? I already know about a window and I'll have a guy there before you open up the shop, okay. Just tell me if you need anything, sweetheart," Billy sounded tired but completely alert.

Charlie was the Sheriff and I guess knows Mister Billy on a first name basis. Sheriff Charlie, Retail Mogul Billy and my mother are all about the same age so I wouldn't be surprised if they didn't all run together as law breaking kids in the nineteen seventies. Mister Billy asked about my mother enough I assumed they knew each other but I've always been too scared to ask *how* they know each other.

"I'm okay Mister Billy," I finally got out, "I think I'm going to go over to my... uhh... my Khai's place to sleep for the next couple nights, maybe. At this point I'm just going to go downstairs and get my baking started for the day. Thank you so much for looking out for me, that's why I love renting from you."

It really did pay off to have a landlord that cared, even if he was doing it for a chance at being with my mom in some capacity. If anything went wrong with the plumbing or central air Billy Bradford always knew a guy that could be there within three hours. Money really does talk in a one Starbucks town like ours.

"I'll see you on Saturday, hopefully? I spoke to Barb earlier this week. She's hired that bartender from Speak Easy on Craven St to make his trademark whiskey drinks for everyone. It's going to be a good show," Billy Bradford boomed through my speaker.

"Yes, I'm baking cookies to pair with the whiskey for dessert, did mom tell you?" I looked at the ceiling, already very bored with this conversation.

"That will be a treat! Well, I'll let you go. I have to call Charlie back. I have arranged for some cars to be on the street and behind in the employee area all day today to keep you save. I gotta protect my girl!" Charlie said in a sing-songy voice.

I narrowed my eyes and my head twisted like a confused puppy. In what capacity was I 'his' girl? *I don't want to know, it's better if I don't know*, I told myself.

"Uh, okay then. Thanks again, Mister Billy. Swing by later this morning and I'll have some of those cream cheese Danish you like, on the house as always," I smiled as I spoke so it would make my voice sound less distressed.

"Of course, dear. I will be there probably around nine thirty to make sure that window got fixed and I want to add alarms to all of your windows while I'm there. Bottom and top floors. Does my code still work on the bottom door? I have a master key for the top," He sounded entirely too cheery for all of this nonsense in the wee early hours of the day.

"Yeah, your code is still active," I said, opening the security app and refreshing it from expired, that's when I realized someone had been playing with the keypad and there had been a string of denied codes on my door about an hour before my window had been cut open.

"I'll talk to you later, okay?" I said again, begging to get off the phone. Billy finally let me get off the phone and I told a nearby cop that I'd like to start baking in the bakery if it was alright.

I went to the bedroom and went ahead and packed myself enough clothes and toiletries for a long weekend. Khai gathered their things in a bag too and we walked downstairs together with a cop in front and a cop behind us.

I recognized Officer Doug from the previous cop encounter and started up some small talk with him. He willingly told me that the crime scene Raleigh guys were here processing trash and the body. Since this business was already on the docket, they responded to the call as well. Clearly, I was the next target.

"Don't scare her, Doug," The cop walking behind us said, "I'm just glad there wasn't any dead bodies on this call if we're being honest here," The cop said with a gagging noise for affect.

"Yeah, I'm glad my girlfriend is a badass, too," Khai said and I stifled a laugh, it was strange to be someone's girlfriend, even though I still didn't know what to call them other than 'my Khai'.

"Hey, I'll go in first and check everything out before everyone goes in, okay? Officer Matthews will hang back with you two until I give the all clear. Understood?" Officer Doug was suddenly all business.

Khai and I bobbed our heads up and down with agreement and we walked over to the employee entrance. I dug around in my bag to fish out the keys and had a hard time finding the right one in the dark until one of the officers shined their flashlight so I could see.

"This is why I normally just walk around the building and go in the front doors," I complained, "It's so hard to see back here."

Officer Matthews looked around the parking lot aiming the flashlight in specific areas.

"There are two street lights out and it looks like the security light back here is broken out. I'll mention it to Billy when he comes by about the one light that he's responsible for. I'll call City of New Bern when they open at eight and get the other ones looked at today before dusk," Officer Matthews he looked down at his phone and I assume was setting up a reminder to get the call made.

Barry was standing behind Officer Matthews chastising me for risking my life and not to mention Khai's life. Barry was going on and on about how I should be more careful and just because he makes it look easy to be in the spirit realm it's not a place I'd want to join before my thread of existence was at its true end.

I tried to acknowledge Barry without Officer Matthews noticing but it didn't work out really well because the police officer looked at me with a super confused expression. He glanced behind himself.

"Do you see anything?" Officer Matthews traded his phone for palming his hand on his weapon, unlatching the strap across the handle.

"I think I saw a bat or something. They love these old buildings. It's nothing," I said, trying to sound natural.

"It's all clear," We heard Officer Doug call from inside the kitchen.

14

Khai pushed the door open completely to let me in but Officer Matthews insisted on being the last one to enter the building. With Khai's help and starting so much earlier I went ahead and made double trays of everything. With all the excitement of the building owner coming, the window guy and the amount of gossip that has been surrounding the Tavern lately I expected this weekend to be just as busy as Tuesday was.

The officers sat in the lobby sipping drip coffee and eating a new pastry as I brought them out. A few of the officers from my apartment started to trickle in when they realized free coffee and pastries were being offered. A few of the officers felt moved to actually pay for their pastries and some fancier coffees and I happily let them do so. By the time Lexi showed up we had been unofficially open for nearly two hours.

"What in holy hell is going on here?" Lexi said, not even trying to be discreet about her language around the full lobby of cops.

A few regulars had decided to come in early too, mainly the people who recognized an officer they knew or customers that simply just wanted to be nosy. I noticed a local reporter milling in the crowd too. All publicity is great for business, I tried to convince myself.

"Someone broke into Eliza's apartment early this morning. She decided to open early because the cops were already coming in here after they processed the scene upstairs. It's been... a morning," Khai looked tired and sounded annoyed at everything in general.

"Holy fuck balls, man," Lexi shoved her bag and jacket in the cubby in the small walkway between the kitchen and the front serving area, "Is this the week from hell or what? I don't know if I can keep up with all of this. You're, okay though, right?"

She turned to me and I just nodded my head up and down, suddenly feeling very tired.

"This *has* been the week from hell. I just want to get on the other side of this so I can sleep for a week straight," I rubbed my palm across the back of my neck and let a yawn escape my lips.

"So, I take it you two are taking off early?" Lexi said, starting to brew her own coffee, "Is Gregor coming in early tonight? Should I call him? I feel like he'd be open to it even though he works all day tomorrow already."

"No, I'll work. I may go upstairs for a few hours and take a nap but I'll be here for my regular shift tonight, if that's okay?" Khai looked at me for approval on all accounts.

"Sure, that sounds like a plan. If it doesn't get too busy here, I'll join you. If It's okay with Lexi. Billy is going to be here in a few hours if he's not already here but upstairs delegating." I sighed.

I filled Lexi in on the full night and for the most part the morning moved on as usual. The flow of customers was a bit more than usual but with three of us we handled it all with ease. To my relief, I had made enough extras of everything that I didn't have to go back in the kitchen at all.

Billy came in with his contractor friend, an electrician and the Sherriff to formally sit down and go over security measures for the entire strip of businesses and a few other locations that Billy Bradford owned.

I understood why I was there for part of the conversation but for a good portion of the whole meeting I just felt tired and zoned out while they discussed properties, I had no opinions about. I even tried to make an excuse to replenish everyone's coffees so I could get up but Lexi had already gotten to the table before I was able to insert myself into the conversation to politely excuse myself.

"You have really built an amazing business here, Miss Woods," the contractor said, with crumbles of my apple turnover falling from his mouth, "Fred always raved about this place but I'm usually working at the other side of town."

"Well, tell Fred I thank him for trying to spread the word of good pastries and good coffee," I smiled although I had no clue who Fred was, "On Tuesday evenings I make a taco pastry and we do trivia, if you ever get over here when you're off the clock."

"That sounds awesome! I'm sure Susan would love that," He said, finishing up his pastry and chasing the bite with his cup of freshly topped coffee.

"My Eliza is just so talented," Billy said, clapping his hands together and adjusting his tie.

I tried not to physically flinch when he referred to me as his but I couldn't help myself. I opened my mouth to protest but he blazed right over me as he continued to talk.

"I know you haven't been back upstairs but I already got that window fixed up and Spencer here will get that equipment set up. You'll have a security camera inside facing that window, in the stairwell and on the outside of the building facing that dreadful fire escape. If you want any more than that just let me know," Billy said in his loud booming voice.

"No, I think that's plenty, thanks. I already have a few cameras in here. I just never really needed any upstairs. I think a lot of people don't even realize that's an apartment up there. Only my employees and the few people I know personally know I live up there. I don't even know how someone would be interested in me. They had to think they were breaking into the business, right?" I said to the table, I surprised myself by the worry in my voice.

"Now don't you worry, Eliza. We're going to get that light in the back fixed up too. I want you to go ahead and disable the code you gave me too because I don't want anyone trying to use it after today," Billy reached over and patted me on the shoulder like we were having a father-daughter moment and suddenly I felt like punching him in the face.

I had no idea what was going on with him lately. He's always been a great landlord and I knew that he had given me a deal on the place because of my mother but he had always been very professional. These last couple interactions have been borderline inappropriate.

I stood up quickly as if remembering something urgent.

"Thank you for that. If you wouldn't mind, I have some paperwork to do in the back that can't wait, pay day stuff. Thanks again for all of this, Mr. Bradford and you too, uh, fellas. Thanks." I turned away from the table before anyone could protest and I walked directly to the back.

I sat down at my small desk in the kitchen and starting breathing through a panic attack. Honestly, I'm shocked it's taken this long for a proper melt down.

I put my forehead down on the edge of the desk and just stared at the grout in between the tiles on the floor. They were the smaller tiles with each little shape being a different color. I had grown accustomed to panic attacks in this kitchen by now so I silently just counted the tiles and tried to decide what color each one was as my eyes glided over them. I inhaled deeply and just let the tears fall from my face. The roaring in my ears was so loud I couldn't hear anything around me.

I jumped when I felt the hand on my back. I looked up and Khai was looking at me with a worried expression across their face.

"Sorry," Khai apologized with full concern dripping from their voice, "you okay?"

I looked up and the tears fell freely from my face and I took a deep breath. Khai waited patiently for me to respond.

"I'll be fine. This is fine. Everything is fine," I grabbed a tissue out of the box I kept on my desk and started cleaning up my face. Even though my eyes were crying I wasn't in full sobs so I was able to pull myself together pretty well. I reapplied my makeup and cleaned up the edges of my eyes the best I could using a pocket mirror.

"This is okay. I'm okay. We're all okay," I said almost convincing myself everything was fine.

"We can stay at my place for the nap instead of your house if that's better for you? I live kind of close, we don't have to go back up to your apartment," Khai was trying to figure out how to properly comfort me and I really wasn't in the mood for it.

"No. Really. I'm fine. I just needed a moment. I'm good now. What's up?" Once my make-up was touched up it was like my emotions never existed. I loved and hated that about myself, "Is Brad and them still here?"

"No, they left already." Khai said, still looking at me like I needed something but they weren't sure what.

"Good. That's better, actually." I did a very long exhale and instantly felt like I could actually make it through the day, "I think I'm going to skip that nap altogether. I'm just going to do a double shot Americano and fight through it."

I tried to smile in a way that was genuine.

Khai's facial expression was full disapproval but they didn't protest when I walked past them to the front and started making my coffee. As the work day dipped into the slow hours Khai excused themselves to run to their own apartment for a nap.

I tried not to let my tiredness bubble up as anger but I couldn't help it. Phoebe had messaged me for lunch plans but I hadn't responded. I just felt like an exposed wire and my sparks were lethal. Whenever I felt like this, I tried to avoid everyone so I wouldn't ruin friendships.

After Khai had left Lexi forced me out of the shop, for her own sanity. I decided to walk around downtown and take a stroll on the water front to clear my mind.

I had reached Union Point Park just as the light turned red going at the cross walk by the draw bridge so I was forced to wait at the intersection while the automated crosswalk beeped at me. I leaned against the pole and forcibly pushed the button five more times than necessary.

"It works the same even if you just push that button once, you know?" I heard a voice say behind me.

I audibly groaned and turned towards the voice to see Lilith standing behind me in a very fancy floor-length flowy black dress and her thick black hair was in Wednesday Adams braids. She looked mildly amused at my presence.

"What do you want?" I finally asked after we stared each other down for a long moment.

"I am here for the Shriners ball when I thought I saw you over here. I just wanted to say hey... and... thank you," Lilith's piousness faded away and suddenly I saw past the faux-goth appearance. I had never really spoken to Lilith at all other than making her cry at Wine Wednesday.

"Thank me? For what?" I tried to keep my aggression down but I know my voice was dripping with sarcasm and anger. I wasn't sure what I was angry at but I was having trouble keeping my voice down.

"For that amazing set up for the funeral. I wasn't allowed to go to his real funeral because of Talbot. He hated that I was in love with Ham. I was honestly amazed that he let us keep meeting on Thursdays but he said that we have to keep up our regular appearances like nothing happened. Talbot's a lawyer, you know. We own an office at the end of this street, actually. I do office work for the firm, which is how I found out that he and Shannon were meeting up without the rest of us. Instead of feeling angry I just called Ham and we ended up developing feelings. Ham was just so easy to talk to, you know? He wasn't like Talbot at all. Talbot always made me feel like an idiot every chance he got while Talbot worshiped me. I was his eternal, you know?"

"Wait, if you all were swapping and lying to each other why did you still hang out as friends? Isn't that awkward? Did Talbot know that you knew about Shannon? What about Shannon's husband? How did Thorny even end up with you all? He's an easy ten years younger than all of you," I was suddenly starting to see where some of the pieces fit together and who could have possibly wanted poor Hammond out of the way.

"Shannon actually had met him on a dating app. She had invited him to your coffee shop since they both went there so much already. I guess she invited him into the core group but told him he would need to bring his own plus one because we were all coupled up. That's when the talk about LARPing public was tossed around. Before we started the vampire group he was coming to our Swingers Nights. We always invited some single people just so we could have some new people in the mix," Lilith cleared her throat.

"Thursdays were the only time I really felt like I was in charge of anything. I am the time keeper and the anointed one. On Thursdays and when I was alone with Ham as myself was the only time that I felt completely whole these days. I would have never risked the group by hurting anyone though. I needed us all there. Talbot would have left me with absolutely nothing if he knew Ham and I were seeing each other outside of Thursday. He also threatened to take our kids and I just... It didn't seem like the risk was worth it. So I stayed with Talbot although my heart belonged to Ham. I better go. Talbot thinks I'm getting something out of the car right now. I'm not sure if we're going to keep doing Thursdays since it was Hammond's idea to begin with, but well, I'll still see you for coffee, okay?" Lilith straightened up and looked around her.

I sighed, suddenly my lack of sleep and near-death experience felt very small in comparison to Lilith's issues. I still didn't even know her real name but I was too awkward to ask. Suddenly I wanted to call Khai and apologize for being... well... myself.

"It's okay," I said, "I believe you. That sounds like a tough situation. You're always welcome to my place for any role playing you have or just for coffee. I'm glad I have customers like you," Somewhere in there I had slipped into manager speak and consumerism.

I loathed that manager tone of voice and phrasing but it was a mechanism I used often while in business to preserve my own sanity within a capitalist system.

Lilith reached out and we thoughtfully held each other's hand for a moment before she walked towards the extended parking lot across the street to retrieve whatever she had faked forgetting out of the car.

I turned towards the intersection and the timer beeped again telling me not to walk, "Ya gotta be fucking kidding me."

I huffed as I pushed the button again.

15

I didn't call Khai during my walk. I couldn't decide what I would say if I did call and I didn't want to risk waking them if they were sleeping. By the time I got back to the Tavern Khai was already sitting behind the counter looking refreshed and freshly showered.

They had changed their clothes and styled their hair. As I walked into the lobby the butterflies bubbled up in my belly and I remembered how my schoolgirl crush had developed originally.

They greeted me as if I was just another customer. I felt a dark cloud come over me. I had upset them more than I had thought.

My brain went back to six years ago when my ex and I were fighting and all the things she put me through to punish me for having emotions that she didn't approve of. I wasn't allowed to be upset, angry or distressed in any way around her. Those emotions just weren't allowed.

I was only allowed to be happy, complacent and helpful when I was with her. I couldn't repeat that torture. If Khai wasn't going to let me process my panic attacks and anxiety in ways that I had figured out worked for me then maybe we weren't going to work out anyway. If Khai didn't want to go to my mom's thing tomorrow then I'd know how they felt, I agreed with myself.

"I think I'm going to go to bed early tonight. You can stay at your house. We haven't really been apart this week. Just let me know if you still want to go to Barb's thing tomorrow. If not, that'll be okay. It's been a long week, hell, a long life and I'm just ready to close my eyes and pretend to be dead for a while." I announced after we stood in awkward silence for longer than ten minutes.

It was just after four o'clock and Gregor would be coming in for the short part of the shift. I didn't need to be a third person on shift since the dining area had boiled down to our regular table top gamers. There was very few beer and wine drinkers whispering about the murder.

I huffed and slammed my apron down on the counter. As I slammed my apron down, I could recognize my actions as a tantrum but I couldn't stop myself.

Khai just stared at me with an expression I couldn't read. I couldn't stand how attracted I was to them and how easily they stayed within the boundaries we had agreed on. No one was that true to their word, were they?

As I got to the door to pull it open, I felt a hand on my shoulder again. Khai had ran up behind me.

"Wait!" Khai called out.

I turned towards them with my hand still on the door. I looked at them without saying anything.

"I got this for you." Khai handed me a small mesh drawstring bag with something hard in it, "It's for protection and stabilizes your connection to the spiritual realm. Or at least that's what the internet says. I got it weeks ago but just never found the right moment to give it to you. When I went home today, I saw it on my dresser and it just felt right. I know you're mad at me or whatever but I'm not ready to quit on you, okay? I'll talk to you tomorrow? Please?" Khai's caramel eyes searched my face to see how I was responding to the gift.

I felt even more like an ass than I did before. I carefully opened the small bag. A thick rough stone of Black Tourmaline mounted with wires twisted around it to hold it into place complete with a black velvet ribbon attached to the stone made it a necklace.

I just stared down at the stone in my hand and then back up at Khai. Why on earth would Khai buy me a gift? Weeks ago? This didn't make any sense. Were they trying to guilt me? Was this a trick? I gulped big and felt my mouth go completely dry.

I wasn't sure if I should fire them outright and then just go on alone until I die or kiss them in front of everyone. My knee-jerk reaction is to push everyone away and lock the door behind me.

The hair stood up on my neck and I felt Barry whisper into my ear, *'Just say 'thank you and we'll talk later' It's that simple, my dear.'*

"Uhhh, thank you and we'll talk later?" I spoke as if my emotions had been turned completely off. Khai just blinked at me.

"Okay. Well, I'll call you when I am doing dishes. If you still don't want me to come up or don't answer because you're asleep I'll understand," Khai sighed and looked back at the barista counter where a teenager was patiently waiting for an employee's return while clutching their empty mug in their hand looking around dramatically.

I nodded still unable to form words. Khai hesitated like there was more to say even though I wasn't contributing to the conversation.

Khai went over to the counter to help the teenager to more caffeine when I offered no response. I glanced over at the table the boy had come from. There was a group of six sitting at the table and laughing together. They had a whole set up of a map in the center of the table and someone was making a miniature of someone's character dance around as they spoke in a funny voice.

One of these days I would have time to join a game again, I thought, *to escape for a few hours to a world that didn't actually exist.*

As I walked up my stairwell, I put the necklace on and rubbed the rough-edged stone. I tried to pull the energy Khai said the black stone processed into my being. If anything, protection was something I was very interested in and maybe if it strengthened the bridge to the spirit world Hammond would be able to say something to me while I was wearing it.

My face and ears were warm from exhaustion and all I wanted to do was lay down in my bed and put a pillow over my head until my alarm went off. I took my shoes off at the door as I walked to the bed room. I pulled off my bra and pants mid-stride. My clothes just fell to the floor in the kitchen on my way to my bedroom. I collapsed onto the bed still wearing my dirty work shirt and curled myself up in a ball. I silenced my phone and plugged it into the charger on the nightstand.

Sleep came to me suddenly.

16

I awoke startled when my alarm went off at three in the morning. The room was completely dark and silent. It didn't even sound like the heat was running.

Between all of the electronics and appliances homes have a baseline hum. My apartment not only had the absence of light, there was also this blatant absence of noise.

I sat up in bed and let my eyes search around the room. My clothes were piled up in the chair and around my dresser. The room didn't have a proper closet but it was connected to the master bathroom. I heard the soft dripping of water from the large claw tub in the bathroom.

It was the very distinct drip, drip noise that startled me. I blinked and tried to focus. Barry manifested and he had his back to the corner of the room, a position that had him looking directly at me but also made it so he could see into the corner of the bathroom where the tub is.

He held a hand up at me as he peered into the bathroom. Why a ghost had to be careful and covert I was unsure but it set me on edge even more.

He slowly made a motion to me to come forward so I could look from his position. I walked over and peered into the bathroom. The curtain was drawn around the tub but there was a dark shadow seated in the tub behind the cream-colored curtain. It looked like someone was taking a bath in my bathtub.

The drip, drip, drip of the water leaking from the tub faucet was so loud it echoed around the room. I couldn't see any blood but it felt like there was blood all over the place, the walls, the curtains, in the water of where the shadow sat in the tub. Everywhere. I could smell the coppery smell of blood in the air.

I couldn't tell if I was actually awake or if this was some type of dream state. I sucked in a deep breath and was startled myself at how loud my breathing was. The head of the shadow turned towards me from the noise. My whole body tensed up. I watched as the shadow pulled back my curtains with bloody fingers to exposed the face of Lilith. Blood pouring from her wrist like small waterfalls.

'You did this to me' ran through my head, *'it was you.'*

I started gasping for breath. I tried to keep eye contact with the shadow version of Lilith. Lilith's figure began to flicker in and out but my own wrists started to burn and ache.

"That's enough!" Barry screamed at the shadow.

I coughed and sputtered bent over trying to catch my breath.

"Message sent, dear lady!" Barry was clapping his hands like he was trying to scare off a bear.

I was down on my knees now still gasping for air.

"Okay, madam, we're done here I said!" Barry approached the shadowy figure swinging his cane angrily at the figure in the tub. The shadow figure finally faded out completely releasing its grip on me.

I sat on the floor for a couple minutes trying to regulate my breathing. By the time I finally got to my feet Barry was gone again. His business was done, I guessed. I approached the tub with caution, the curtain was still pulled. Personally, I always kept the curtain pulled open because these types of scenarios freaked me out completely.

I slowly pulled the curtain back all the way to see a completely full tub of water. The faucet dripped twice and I almost lost my footing from jumping. I reached down and pulled the plug so the water could drain out, I made sure to tighten the faucet handles so the dripping would stop.

Once all the water had drained and the distressed spirit had completely separated its self from my apartment, I lit a small cone incense of lavender in the bathroom. I also lit a votive candle I had etched a cleansing spell into. I put the candle in a votive holder so it wouldn't burn the building down while I got ready for work.

By the time I had worked up the courage to unlock my phone I was running thirty minutes behind. Khai had called and left a voice mail a few minutes shy of eight o'clock the previous night. I had also missed a few text messages about an hour after that but not an excessive amount.

I read the text messages as I walked into the kitchen. Khai apologized more for things that they weren't really at fault for in the messages.

Now that I had a well-rested brain, I felt like complete shit about how I had acted the previous day. Khai didn't deserve someone like me, they deserved much better.

I rubbed my face with my hands and decided against my regular make up today. I just did enough foundation so I didn't look sick and some eye liner. I didn't even do mascara today or lipstick. I dug out the THC lip balm I had in the fridge and coated my lips up. Yep, it was going to be one of those days.

I played the voicemail while I descended the steps, Khai was saying that they hoped I was sleeping well and not just ignoring them because yesterday was weird when someone loudly knocked on the outer door. I froze with my hand on the door and waited.

The abrupt knocks turned into aggressive pounding on the door. I looked around the stairwell, there was literally nothing in there but me and my phone.

Where the hell did Barry go? The person on the other side of the door started jiggling the handle while still pounding on the door at the same time. I just stood there unsure of what to do.

What if it was the intruder? Or not even a real person but a spirit trying to get in after I blessed the apartment? Spirits have manifested themselves to me like this before. Living in my world it was sometimes hard to tell what was tangible and what was astral.

Hammond's face appeared in the door and the knife wasn't in his head anymore. He even looked pretty normal to me compared to last few times he projected himself to me. He mouthed the word *"No"* to me.

I pulled my hand away from the door and sat down on the steps, casually flipping through my phone numbers to find Chad. I knew if I called, he would show up no matter what the time of day. If this ended up being a real police matter then I was still calling the police, right?

"Yeah, babe?" He said after two rings.

"I'm not your babe. There is someone banging on my door like a maniac. Could you come over here or call someone?" I started digging through the canvas bag I used as a purse and found a small bag of THC gummies that had been long lost in the clutter of my bag. I popped one in my mouth.

"They don't seem like they can get in but they aren't stopping either," I said just as the pounding started again. If Chad could hear it then this was a real person furiously trying to get into my apartment.

I could hear movement through the phone. Chad was talking to someone else in the room.

"Yeah, I'll call Doug. I think he's on the clock already and his beat is downtown. I'll get there when I can," The line went dead.

Love you too, sweetie, I mused as I ate another gummy.

The banging suddenly stopped and I pressed my head to the door to see if I could hear if Officer Doug had arrived to save me.

It was hard to hear anything at all. After what felt like ages, I decided it was time to open the door. I slowly turned the door handle after unlocking the deadbolt and swung open the door.

I was still chewing the gummy when a hooded figure, the same hooded figure that had broken into my apartment, stepped into the street light.

17

"Um, Shannon? Is that you?" I took a wild guess. I had a hunch it was either Shannon or Talbot himself that was causing all of this trouble.

"You already took care of Lilith so now it's my turn? Is that the deal?" I called out towards the figure. They just stood there and twisted the handle of the knife they had in their hand so I could see the glint of the blade as it hit the street light from above.

For a long while we just stood there, staring at each other. The gummies were starting to work and I was feeling pretty astral myself.

"Well, if you aren't going to kill me can I go to work now?" I called out, holding back a laugh.

My life was in clear peril and I was cracking jokes. I needed to email my therapist to see if they have references for someone closer in my area I could speak to.

"Well, okay then. Happy killing, I guess!" I waved to the hooded person and that's when the figure went in full sprint towards me.

The door had already closed behind me to my stairwell and I heard the automatic deadbolt lock. My keys were lost in my bag somewhere. My best bet was to take off running towards the street and hope Officer Doug was nearly here already.

I started to run around the building when Hammond appeared making me stop my tracks. He pointed away from the bakery in the opposite direction. I turned on my heels to run where Hammond was pointing just as the cop car came around the corner and clipped the hooded figure, cutting them off.

The hooded figure spun around and a leg went freely in directions bones aren't organically meant to bend. Officer Doug got out of the car along as two more cop cars pulled up behind him. Their vehicles cut off the square between the buildings on both sides and blocked the road. An ambulance and fire trucks showed up second later. Chad had called an all-alarm response.

I walked over to the hooded figure who was grabbing at their leg as they laid on the brick pathway of the square where the car had launched them.

If I had kept running in the direction I had originally took off in, the cop car might have hit me instead. I bent down at a safe distance to see if I could figure out who was trying to attack me.

To my shock it was Shannon's husband. His hood had fallen back in the fall and he was yelling obscenities at me. Doug was walking over when Shannon's husband was confessing his crimes.

"You stupid bitch!" he yelled, "If you could have just kept your nose in your own goddamned business! If you had just let me kill you yesterday." He grunted and reached down to his leg, "If Shannon hadn't started fucking that little gamer boy. I had to kill him because he was ruining our lives. We had a great thing going before he got there. I was finally getting into Talbot's circle and his wife was starting to help me ruin him!" He screamed in pain and started reaching around for his knife.

I sprinted over the short distance and kicked the blade away from him. He lunged at me but his leg stopped him before he could get to me.

"Why did you kill Hammond? Why put him in my dumpster?" I asked just as Officer Doug reached us both.

"It was your damn coffee shop that started it all. Shannon met that asshole there and then Talbot insisted we meet there for that stupid vampire shit. I was doing all of this to save my marriage but all it was doing was driving us farther apart. All because of you and your fucking nerd shit," He hissed.

I took a step back while the EMTs put him on a stretcher on wheels. Officer Doug started reading him his rights while cuffing him to the stretcher. Shannon's husband, who I still didn't know what his name was, screamed names at me in between cussing at the EMTs and the assisting police officers.

18

I started baking cookies as soon as I was able to get to the kitchen. Cookies were the fastest things I could get out front and I was starting terribly late to be able to be ready for my mom's thing this afternoon.

Gregor would be coming in any minute now this morning and I've barely gotten anything done. Luckily the cops didn't want to come in for free coffee this time so I was able to lock the door behind me and get to baking. It was really difficult for me to stay focused while the cops were talking to me because I was really, really stoned. Chad had showed up right as I brought the first tray of cookies out so I let him in the front door.

He hugged me tight. I just let him embrace me for a long moment. In the moment, I really needed the hug.

"I'm so glad you're okay," he said, stroking the tips of my hair with his fingers.

I pulled back and leaned even farther back when he went in for a kiss.

"Sorry, bro. Not today," I started giggling because I realized I had used the word 'bro' in a sentence non-ironically.

"Are you high?" He said in full disgust, "You know that's not legal in North Carolina."

"You going to arrest me, officer?" I said, moving farther away from him, "Or are you going to eat some free cookies as a thank you and be on your way? Can you do me a favor and check on Talbot and his wife? I think something is wrong there and I just want to make sure Lilith, or whatever her real name is, is okay," I was already shoving cookies in a paper bag by the time he met me at the opposite side of the barista counter.

"I'll get the cookies and go check on Mrs. Chandler but you need to be careful with that stuff. You've got a lot to lose these days," Chad said in his best friend voice, apparently excusing my dismissal of him because of two attempts on my life, "Just look around you. You are so successful and amazing. I just wish you'd see it. I came in here to see if you were okay and tell you I was sorry about that kiss the other day. I didn't want them to see my face and I've always wanted to do that like in the movies. Have a great day, Miss Woods."

He yanked the bag out of my hand and turned around to storm out. I just watched him go. I waited until he was completely gone before I went over to relock the door behind him.

Chad could be sweet when he wanted to but it was really hard to trust him. When I had called earlier he answered with a pet name but I heard the girl in the background. *I will not fall for his blue eyes this time,* I promised myself.

I immersed myself in getting the baking done in the back. At least I had been able to get a lot of prep done the night before otherwise this morning would be even worse.

Gregor came in a few minutes early and helped me bring some trays out. My high was starting to fade and I realized that Khai might be awake for me to call them. I put my last batch of Baby muffins into the oven and called Khai.

"Hello, Khai's phone," A girl answered with a little giggle.

I looked down to my phone to make sure I had called the right number. Then it registered that the voice had actually said Khai's phone. I checked the time and it was barely eight in the morning, who the hell was Khai with this early in the morning? I pressed the red hang up button on the screen and put the phone back in my pocket.

I felt like puking up my breakfast and went to sit down at my desk until the baking timer went off. I mindlessly started doing the paperwork for getting everyone's paycheck to them. That's when I decided that I did need to let Khai go.

It was getting too complicated with them being my employee and romantic interest and I really needed to keep those aspects of my life better separated. I couldn't quit working here so the only other option was them working somewhere else. I'd even help them find a job elsewhere.

My phone started ringing for the fifth time in a row. Khai's name flashed across the screen and I swiped to silence it. They were leaving another voice mail.

"Eliza, a lady is here and says you agreed to bake cookies for her boss? You don't have to get up, I'll grab them. What kind was it? Have they paid?" Gregor was glancing around my extra messy kitchen this morning and raised an eye brow as I swiped to ignore Khai's eighth call.

"Oh, that would be one of my mom's henchmen. Ring them up on my account and I'll get the cookies together. I have them cooked already just not put in boxes. It's two hundred red velvet chocolate chip cookies," I got up from the chair right when the oven timer went off and I got back to work.

By the time I had gotten to the front I saw Khai walking through the lobby door and I turned back into the kitchen, making them chase me to the back.

"I have to explain. Did you get my voicemails?" Khai looked like they had rushed over immediately and they were already holding their work shirt in their hand, twisting it anxiously.

"Are you holding your shirt because you're quitting?" I asked simply, the numbness was creeping in.

"Well, yes, but that has nothing to do with Tiff answering my phone. She yanked the phone off of the top of my car when she heard it ring. We met up to give each other our stuff back from when we were together. She did that as a power play just to get under your skin. She got access to my phone when I was putting my stuff in my car from hers. It was dumb. I just put my phone up there out of habit. These pants don't have fucking pockets! I don't know. It just happened so fast and then you wouldn't answer your phone. I know it looked bad. I know your ex was a cheating asshole. I just... I don't know what to do," Khai paused to breath.

I just stared blankly unsure if I should believe this version of the story or not. I hated feeling played and lied to. I didn't want to think Khai was just like everyone else I had dated.

"You don't have to turn your shirt in, you know. I gift those to everyone that works here. I take it you're not working out a notice?" I said flatly, choosing anger instead of despair.

"I want to. I do. I will. I can," Khai spoke in rushed broken sentences.

"Then do that but don't be surprised if I'm not going to help you too much through your shifts. I will ask Lexi or Gregor to help cover. Now if you'll excuse me, I have to go clean my kitchen so I can go to this dinner at my mother's house... *alone*. I need to adjust to just always being alone," I turned away from Khai and started cleaning my counters off.

I was loading dishes into the industrial dish washer when I realized that Khai had never left. They were sweeping and started the mop water. We both cleaned the kitchen in silence, staying a comfortable distance away from each other. I did my best to avoid all eye contact and when there was nothing left to clean, I took my apron off and threw it in the laundry basket used for company linens.

We just stood there staring at each other in silence. I crossed my arms across my chest keeping an annoyed expression. Khai looked painfully uncomfortable.

"Why did you help me clean?" Was all I could come up with to say.

"I stayed because I was going to work up the nerve to tell you why I'm putting in my notice but you didn't seem to be in the mood for conversation," Khai replied, trying to step closer to me.

I stepped back every time they took a step forward.

"If we aren't going to work out and you're going back to Tiff I don't want to even bother with the pleasantries. You can just go and I'll figure it out. I've had people walk out on me before. I always bounce back and the business keeps going," I tried to keep my voice steady.

"I'm quitting because my computer business is doing really well and I don't have to work here to pay my bills anymore. I'd rather just be your romantic partner and that's it. I don't want to twist our lives together in a way that you get bored of me too soon. I also don't want you to feel like we have to be a certain way when we're both in the Tavern on the clock or off, okay? I know you're weird about it and from a professional stand point. I get it. The only reason why I stayed here even though my internet business was flourishing was to help save up extra cash so I could buy a house that I want to double as a home base for my business," Khai paused to see if I was still actively listening.

They shifted their weight from one leg to the other and sighed heavily.

"My realtor called me at seven this morning to tell me that my offer got accepted," Khai spoke with urgency, "I noticed that Tiff had texted me after I hung up with the realtor and it just worked out that I could meet up at her apartment on the way over here. I wanted to come right over and tell you about the new place. I didn't want to wait in telling you that I'd work long enough to train my replacement. I can finally get my shit out of storage and spend a lot more time building my business in an actual office space. No more renting a room in a house that doesn't belong to me. I will finally be able to have a real space that is just mine and an office space for my business. Being self-employed makes it nearly impossible to get a house lease around here no matter how much money you have to put down."

"That's also why I always flirted with you and encouraged your flirting because I knew my time as your employee had an end date," Khai added, "I love you. I've *been* in love with you. Tiff was a distraction that didn't work out. It was a dick move getting her a job here but I thought it would redirect my attention and I was just shitty for it. I honestly can't apologize enough for that. I guess I was bitter because after we had hooked up that last time you basically told me to just be your employee or quit. I thought about that conversation a lot. An awful lot. I don't want to be your employee anymore. I want to be the person you are able to relax with and roll dice with. I want to come here and sit in the lobby and sip coffee with you while you're on your break. Okay? We have an electricity that I've never felt before. I can't ignore it anymore. I won't ignore it anymore. I don't want anything standing in the way for how I feel about you."

I almost wanted to burst into applause for how passionate Khai's speech was. I recalled that conversation a lot too but I remembered it differently. I remembered us discussing the whole boss and employee dynamic and how awkward it was. I felt like I was taking advantage of them no matter how much they said I wasn't. It felt dirty and I hated how guilty it made me feel. Emotionally, I wasn't ready to be romantically involved with anyone at that time last year and those emotions obviously took charge in that conversation. *I have apologizing to do too,* I decided.

"Thank you for telling me all of that. I agree that things would be less weird between us if I wasn't your boss anymore. I'm really happy that your business is taking off. I'm glad that I could help you buy a place of your own, even if it was from a paycheck point of view. I'm not good with all this emotions stuff. My ex didn't let me have emotions, to be honest. I thought you were mad at me because of my panic attack," I confessed. I leaned back against the counter behind me and bit my lip ring nervously.

"What? Never! You can't control those. I know that," Khai said sounded fully offended and a little bit confused.

"I remember in that conversation you saying that you didn't want to work in a coffee shop for the rest of your life. You said it in a way that made me think that you thought you are better than me," I said, biting down on the ring in my lip for real this time. I flinched from the pain.

"You own this place. I am just an employee. That's what I meant. Unless you were going to make me part owner, which I'm not interested in, there is no reason for me to invest myself here in that way," Khai sounded annoyed. I wondered if they still felt like they loved me.

"Understood," I said plainly. Awkwardly I yanked at my hair tie to let my hair down. I suddenly had a headache.

"Okay, okay. So, if I'm understanding this properly," I rubbed my temples as I spoke, "we're romantically okay and you'll help me find your replacement in no established amount of time but sooner is better than later. Tiff is still a horrible monster human that should be destroyed. You've been in love with me this entire time and *you* were actually pursuing *me* this entire time so I have nothing to feel guilty about?" I scratched at my scalp where the tight bun was and tried my best to breath in and out like a normal person.

"Pretty much." Khai said, taking a step closer to me, "So we're okay now?"

"I didn't say we were okay," I said plainly. Khai moved closer to me and I didn't step away this time, "But I am open to figuring this all out. This has just been a really fucking weird week. Someone was trying to kill me this morning."

Khai's whole body now leaned against mine and was leaning towards me for a kiss while I spoke. We were nearly the same height. With my thick soled kitchen shoes on it was hard to decide who was the taller out of the both of us.

Khai paused and pulled their head back.

"What?" Khai asked without removing their arms around my waist.

"I have a lot to fill you in on," I said before planting a kiss on their lips, "But we can talk later before Barb's dinner party."

19

"I have no words." Khai said as I stepped out of my bedroom wearing a dark purple sweater dress.

My long black hair was down and let it hang down past my shoulders in the wavy mess it did naturally. I had pinned a few strands of hair that wouldn't get out of my face back with a little skull beret.

I was wearing stockings that had a lace pattern that stop right above my knee so my legs wouldn't get cold. My fitted faux-leather boots stopped halfway up my shin. My eyeshadow matched the color of the dress. I wore my three regular necklaces and the new necklace Khai had given me. My black and white linen scarf hung open draped across my shoulders. The scarf felt just obnoxious enough to piss my mother off.

The sweater dress had short sleeves but I was warm with the scarf and boots. My tattoos of skulls, tombstones and Barry's family crest were easily visible on my arms. I even had a little bear tattoo of the Bern bear on the back of arm near my elbow. As much as I hated this place I grew up in, I was beginning to embrace this city for everything it was. Ghosts and murderers alike.

Khai stood up and I smiled at what they were wearing. Khai wore dark suit pants that were very fitted and slick black shoes with a very obnoxious blouse. A dark black scarf with a chunky knitted jacket with a thick belt through the middle tied it all together. The entire outfit was a perfect blend of masculine and feminine energies. Khai didn't wear any make up tonight and left their face unshaven so a soft stubble had formed.

"Are you ready to suffer through a horrible night with the richest people in our town?" I wrapped my arm around theirs and we reached the bottom of the stairs right as Phoebe approached us in her normally flowy garb and Lexi a few steps behind.

Lexi was wearing a tight black dress and holding a satin name brand clutch that coordinated with her very tall heels. Her long blonde hair was curled instead of straightened.

"I hope you don't mind that I invited Lexi," Phoebe said once we were closer, "Isn't she just gorgeous?" Phoebe took a step back to really look at her date for the night.

Khai quickly looked at the couple before us and then back to me.

"What did I miss?" Khai exclaimed.

"Oh yeah, Lexi and Phoebe are together now," I said, forgetting that I had completely forgotten to mention it.

"Well, I'm glad you can keep a secret, Eliza," Phoebe laughed, "At least secrets about other people's loves lives that is."

Everyone laughed at my expense and I couldn't help but laughed too. In a small town any secret feels huge when it's uncovered.

We all loaded up in Phoebe's SUV. Phoebe drove us to my mother's house with my help from the back seat.

"Holy shit, you didn't tell me you were rich, Eliza," Phoebe gasped once we got through the entry gate. I had to get out of the vehicle to push in a code to get us through.

"I'm not rich. My mom is," I insisted.

"This house is massive," Lexi said bending down to look at the full house before we slowed near where a temporary valet area was set up.

Phoebe took a ticket in exchange of her keys and I saw my friends all exchanging glances at my expense.

"You grew up in this house?" Khai asked as they laced their fingers into mine at the base of the large stone steps.

"Yep. I went to a public school just like everybody else. I never invited anyone to my house for any reason because of this response. There is a lot of money in this small town that people just don't see because it's behind gates," I tried to downplay how extravagant my childhood home was to no avail.

"You had me thinking you were struggling to make ends meet at the coffee house. Why have we not expanded more and got new chairs for the dining room yet?" Lexi asked once she caught up with us at the top of the stairs.

"Again, I am not rich. My mother is," I insisted, "I have a trust fund but it can't be accessed until I'm forty-five. It's to force me to 'live honestly' or so my mother says. She also said it was so I wouldn't marry for the wrong reasons. Or at all."

"We are old maids," Lexi said, "all my friends are on their second or third kid already."

"And second or third marriages," Phoebe inserted with a laugh.

"You'll understand a lot more about where I came from after this party. You've all seen my mother in public. You will see her in a private setting tonight. Brace yourself," I lead the way through the front door.

Once we were officially in the house the audible gasps from my friends were hard to ignore. There were caterers rushing around with drink orders with small hors d'oeuvres on big silver platters.

This would be the first time I arrived to one of my mother's soirees on time and with friends. With a support system I was better mentally prepared to take on the room. I had survived two murder attempts and helped solve a murder, this dinner couldn't be nearly as painful as all that, right?

20

We walked farther into the large foyer and Khai squeeze my arm closer to them. I thought it was nervousness about approaching a large room full of overdressed people but then an older man I didn't recognize came up and shook hands with Khai. They quickly started talking software and other computer related subjects. Khai introduced the man as Jordan Blackman, a local computer repair business owner and that they had met at the coffee shop.

Apparently, this man was a regular at my shop. I thanked him for supporting my business and after a few pleasantries I was very bored with their conversation so I excused myself to Phoebe and Lexi.

My best friend and her new romantic partner had a group around them talking lively in between bursts of laughter. My friends fit right into this crowd and suddenly I felt very victimized.

How is it so easy for them to merge with this crowd? Okay, so Lexi and Phoebe were cut from the same cloth these people were so it wasn't a bit stretch but selfishly I had hoped that Khai would be attached to me most of the night. I grabbed a glass off of a passing waiter's tray and drank its entire contents in a full gulp.

"You might not want to get too drunk in public," a deep male voice said out of my eyesight. I turned towards the voice and it was Sheriff Charles Hardy, "You've had a rough week. I wouldn't want to add some type of public intoxication charge to it."

"Well, I'm not in public so I'll be fine," I said plucking a second glass off a nearby table and downing it too, "I'm also not driving, Pheebs is my driver tonight."

I smirked, drinking the last from the glass before casually walking off to the small bar that is a permanent installation in the living room. My mother had hired the bartender from a bar downtown to serve everyone.

"Hey Jake, can I get the stout and a shot of whatever the most expensive liquor my mother has provided for tonight," I smiled broadly knowing that the sheriff was still watching me closely.

The bartender obliged and I was about to take the shot when Sheriff Hardy caught up with me.

"I know you're in a mood tonight but I wanted to talk to you about your involvement in the Hammond Fletcher case," the Sheriff paused just long enough for me to swallow the shot and shove a tip in the jar, "You also tipped off Deputy Jones about Maryanne Chandler and I need to know how you knew she was bleeding out in her tub."

I gulped my beer and successfully didn't choke on it although I wasn't sure I couldn't get it down at first.

"Is she okay?" I asked once the beer was safely down my throat. Purposely avoiding his actual question.

"Barely. They airlifted her to Pitt and she's not in the green yet. We have Mister Chandler in custody and their kids are with her parents until we can figure out what happened. She kept repeating your name to the emergency personnel in the ambulance on the way to the hospital, you know?" He said before sipping on his own whiskey neat. For extra emphasis he leaned into the conversation so those around us wouldn't hear.

I didn't respond with words. I just drank another long gulp from my pint glass.

"Why would she be saying your name? What did you have invested in this group of vampire weirdos?" Sheriff Charles pressed harder.

I took a physical step back although he hadn't really gotten closer to me with his leaning.

"I checked you out," he continued, "you haven't even had a speeding ticket since high school and the only other charges were filed by you and not against you. Does your employee play thing know what you've been through?"

"Khai isn't going to be my employee much longer. What do you care about my love life anyway? What are you getting at? I don't believe I'm under arrest for anything so you got nothing on me, sir," I said 'sir' in the most sarcastic way possible. My glass was nearly empty from nervously drinking it with every word Sheriff Hardy spat in my direction.

"I need to figure you out. I want to know how you know things. Who is your informant?" Sheriff Hardy insisted.

"I just own a nerdy coffee shop, okay? I make muffins with eggs in them and eight hundred cookies a day. That's all I know," I finished my beer and sat it back down on the counter motioning for a refill from the bartender before turning back to the Sheriff.

"Look," I said feeling fueled by liquid courage, "I know you're trying mega hard to intimidate me right now but we're in my mother's house. My old bedroom is upstairs. This is my home turf and I have the upper hand. You can just fuck off, sweetie. I don't have the energy for this. If you really want to help me then do things that are important. You should really get your guys to respond to shit faster. I had to bash a dude in the head with a tequila bottle so he wouldn't murder me in my bed. I feed all your guys free shit constantly so maybe they'll care about me enough to save my life in the future. Life is short, okay? Let's just cut the shit."

I took a sip from my refreshed pint glass and I could feel that the sheriff was bracing himself although his facial expression remained neutral.

"I see ghosts, alright," I said a little too loudly, "Bartholomew Digby is buried in Cedar Grove Cemetery, look him up. He is my informant. He died a few hundred years ago at that old school that was used as a hospital downtown. He tells me a bunch of shit I'd rather never know about. Before you accuse me of anything, you know my mother. She's had me tested and I've been to the best psych wards in the country. I'm not schizophrenic and I'm not delusional. I have a double Master's degree in business and sociology. I have nothing to prove to you. Now if you'd excuse me, I want to go fuck my date in my childhood bedroom," I raised my glass to him and stormed off towards Khai.

I almost burst out laughing or maybe hysterically crying at his audacity but I managed to hold it together until I got to the other side of the room.

I didn't actually have plans on dragging Khai upstairs to my old bedroom immediately but I have fantasized about it a few times just to get me through the evening.

Other than being accosted by Sheriff Charles Hardy, the night went pretty well. My mother was in a pleasant mood and really spoke highly of my business. She made sure to embarrass me by making me stand up and explain the cookies like they were a science project but it gave me the opportunity to plug the coffeeshop.

As much as I hate it, networking is the only way to survive in a small town. Public speaking isn't my forte but I managed to get everything out that I wanted to say and excuse myself to the whiskey drink of the night before my mother took over the emcee duties to introduce a local jazz band to finish off the night with dancing.

For this to be a dinner party there wasn't much actual food, I noted. I was pretty intoxicated before the end of the night.

21

I woke up the next day with a loud pounding on my temples and to my distress I was in my childhood bedroom. Khai was twisted up in the sheets, I looked down and was fully clothed.

I tried to remember how the night panned out but after my speech went my memory gets very fuzzy. We rode together with Phoebe and Lexi so there wasn't a driving fear if we left.

Did I decide we stay the night? Or was I just so drunk it was easier to put me to bed while the party went on? I rubbed my face completely ignoring the amount of makeup that was still smeared across my face.

I shambled to the connecting bathroom like the undead in a black and white movie and started the shower. *After a shower I will do things,* I promised myself. Khai barely stirred from the sound of the shower coming from the bathroom.

I chugged water from an unopened water bottle that had been left on my nightstand. I took three pain relief pills from the medicine cabinet behind my bathroom mirror. I braced myself over the sink as a wave of nausea washed over me.

After getting naked I slipped into the brisk shower. A cool shower after a night of drinking always helped me the most. No amount of sports drink or headache medicine could do what a cold shower does to me after drinking too much.

I froze when I realized that I wasn't alone in the shower. I slowly slid down the slick tile wall until my bottom was resting on the floor of the shower. Mist fell freely around me.

The small-framed girl hunched at the opposite end of the large shower was being hit by the water directly but her image barely wavered. I knew on many levels that this small girl wasn't a part of the living.

The spikes being driven into my skull had to be ignored for a few moments while I tried to keep my cookies down and figured out what message was being sent to me.

"You're safe here," I said to the transparent brown haired girl. The girl looked up confused, the water going through her shadowy figure and the mist of the water only occasionally stuck to her hair and face before bouncing into the air once more.

"Can I help you? I can feel that you're afraid. You're being kept somewhere against your will," I pressed my palms against my temples trying to press the hangover pains back.

"Wait, this isn't hangover pain, is it? Someone hit you with something heavy. On your temple," I felt the shower water trickle down my face but from this young girl's memory I had the sensation that my eye was bleeding.

I blinked away water droplets forming in my eyelashes. The angelic face of the young girl before me became very disfigured and her whole body was smeared with dirt. She wasn't a young adolescent girl at all, but late teens or early twenties instead.

Her whole body was smeared with blood and mud. Her hair was chopped off on one side and her eye was completely caved in. The image of the young woman seemed to grow in size. I shrank back against the shower wall to avoid touching her growing aura of pain and despair.

I was still sitting at the bottom of the shower when Khai opened the glass door stepping directly where the young girl once was. I reached out but the ghastly presence dissolved immediately.

"Holy shit it's cold in here!" Khai proclaimed withdrawing their leg instinctively.

"Oh yeah, that's my hangover cure. The coldest shower I can stand," I forced a smiled as I stood up carefully. The pain in my face had subdued greatly.

"I wouldn't have tried to get in here but the amount of fog on the mirror made me think that it was boiling hot in here! I saw the message you wrote so I thought you wanted me to join you," Khai stood there, completely naked contemplating actually joining me or not due to the temperature of the water.

"Message? What?" I turned the knob in the shower to make the water warmer and looked past Khai to the mirror and saw the words, 'FIND ME' written in the fogged-up kitchen mirror.

"Huh. Well, the water should be better for you now. I'm actually not as hungover as I thought," I took a step back and let the water run over me as Khai joined me. I couldn't help but smile at the ease of our budding relationship.

"So... you didn't write that?" They said, "Is that GHOST writing?" Khai's eyes grew large.

A few minutes later we were drying off with fluffy brand-new towels that surprisingly didn't smell like dust from sitting unused for a long period of time. This house had a knack for keeping things pleasant. Although this house was the size of a small museum it still had familiar smells that brought me comfort.

I dug through my dressers trying to find something we could both wear for our trip back to my apartment. I chose my old track sweats that had NBHS printed on the legs and across the belly with my last name printed on the back.

E. Garver - The Java Tavern Series: Fangs & Fiends

Khai was sporting an old Mumfest shirt from the two thousand and seven and some large basketball shorts. My wardrobe always consisted of an androgynous mix of clothes.

Luckily, I also had old foam flipflops we could both wear. Wearing dress shoes first thing in the morning with yesterday's socks just didn't sound pleasant to either of us.

Turns out we have the same shoe size and Khai claimed my purple flip-flops saying I'd only ever see them when they wore them in front of me from this day on. We laughed about Khai's flip flop theft on our way down the stairs, juggling our clothes from the night before in our arms.

"Dear, please meet me in the kitchen," my mother's voice bounced off the large foyer walls although she was nowhere to be seen.

Khai decided to wait by the front door and get us an uber while I spoke to my mother. I unceremoniously dropped my armload to the floor near Khai's feet.

I knew that my mother was in the kitchen so that's where I headed. She was sipping her coffee casually in the booth style breakfast table under a large window. Her live-in maid was busying herself cleaning up remnants of last night's party.

"Would you like some tea or coffee, dear?" My mom broke the silence.

"Uhh, no. I'm good, thanks," I shifted nervously from one foot to the other.

"You made quite the spectacle last night," My mom still hadn't met my eyes yet, she was reading from a Charlotte Gazette newspaper. Her body language was barely even acknowledging my presence, "You have a visitor. Sit."

I sat obediently at the barstool she had motioned to across from the breakfast table she was sitting at.

"I gotta go, Mom. Khai is getting us an uber. I'm not sure how long we'll have to wait for it," I feigned urgency trying to escape the awkwardness of being alone with my very polished mother at seven in the morning.

"It takes Uber at least fifteen minutes in this town and that's if you're lucky that someone is online. Calm down, dear. You've got time for this," She cleared her throat.

I tried not to think about why my mother would ever need an uber when I heard the half bath door open from the hall and Sheriff Charles came through the threshold of the kitchen. He was fighting with his police utility belt as he walked.

Sheriff Charles Hardy was in full uniform and I could see the little drops of water from him washing his hands on the edge of his wrists.

I opened my mouth to speak but before I could say a word, my mother raised her hand, palm forward, to stop me.

"The spectacle I mentioned was about Charlie here. He asked to verify some information you gave him last night and sadly, I obliged. You've always been a good girl and kept out of trouble, which is the only reason why I gave this information willingly. And the fact that it's Charlie. We go way back," My mom paused to turn towards the police sheriff and smiled coyly at him before turning back to me, "Now if you'll excuse me. If you need me, I am now retiring to my office to get a jump on the week. You two talk. I'll see you on Monday when I meet the girls for coffee, Dear," My mother finally looked me in the eye and gave me a strange nod, "And Charlie, I'll see you Friday night." She strode over and kissed him on the cheek.

I tried to act like this whole thing was normal. Since when did my mother have Friday nights with the fucking police sheriff?! I also had instant regret using the world 'fucking' in the same sentence of mother and sheriff. I decided to remain silent due to the violence happening in my mind. I just looked at the sheriff dumbly. I felt like I was a teenager again and I was dressed for the part.

"Miss Woods, I'm here as a professional but we're off the books until you give me something solid, understood?" Sheriff Charles walked over to a briefcase that I hadn't noticed before and pulled out a short stack of manila folders.

Each folder had pictures paper clipped to the front of them. I counted four faces.

"These are victims of a serial murder case that has gone cold. According to our resources in Raleigh this guy is about to hit again and we have found evidence that ties these victims together but we're missing bodies. We really could use any leads at all," He slid the files in my direction.

"Show these to no one. In fact, you stole them off of my desk while I wasn't looking. Okay?" He placed his business card on top of the stack, "You call me if this gives you vibes or whatever. I'll follow any lead you give me at this point. Your mother assures me that you're legit and she even offered to let me read your medical file if it made me feel more comfortable working with you. I've known you for years and I had heard some rumors but I never knew.... I--uhh know you've had trouble in your past. This doesn't go unappreciated, Eliza. You give me good leads and we'll come to an arrangement. I already have the mayor on standby and I'm ready to grease some wheels for you."

I sat there for a long moment before I allowed my exhale to escape my lips.

"Okay. But I'm a ghost. No one knows it's me helping," I said without touching the files.

"Agreed." He clapped his hands together once, "You won't regret this. I have full faith in you."

Internally everything in my stomach turned to mush and I felt bile creep up from the depths of my soul. I know I'm helping victims but the fact that I'm going to be paid off by favors via the mayor just made me feel dirty. What type of favors do they think I'll want to cash in? I just clutched the files to my chest and excused myself, running quickly to Khai.

"You okay, love?" Khai asked while pushing the door open.

I rushed past them without glancing back in the direction of the kitchen. Luckily Khai was able to carry both piles of our clothes with poise while I pulled the envelopes so close to my body, they almost fused to me entirely.

"I'm alright. I just feel like I agreed to something I don't understand the magnitude of, that's all," I crawled into the uber driver's back seat and tried to ignore the ghost lawn keeper trimming the bushes that outline the driveway.

What did I just agree to? Why is the mayor involved?

Epilogue

"Should we say something special?" Phoebe asked our small group.

We stood in a half circle around Barry's tombstone. We were all dressed in darker shades of colors like you would a regular funeral. I thought dressing the part was a kind gesture from my friends.

The stone marker was so old it was nearly impossible to read the name if you didn't already know what it was.

I had already reached out to a volunteer tombstone cleaner to come out and clean it up thoroughly. Now that the moss stains and dirt were washed away it almost looked like new.

I was still holding the wreath. Phoebe, Lexi and Khai accompanied me because we plan on going to dinner after. Like you would a real funeral, you know.

There is lore that if you go to any type of celebration of life in a place surrounded by death you must stop somewhere as an errand or eat at a restaurant before returning home. Otherwise, an angry spirit may follow you home. Or the deceased themselves will cling to you out of sadness of being dead.

"I say enough to Barry as it is," I joked.

Barry manifested behind his tombstone. He was wearing fancier clothes than the fancy clothes he typically wears. I didn't know that was possible. He was wearing a gold necklace with his family's British crest pressed into it. His gloved hand was wrapped around the crest while the other rested on the top of his tombstone. His head was slightly bowed. The expression on his face was somber.

"Bartholomew Digby has been my best friend since I was a little girl," I started the eulogy, "Confused by my capabilities as a person. Desperate to find a connection with anyone that didn't think I was a monster. Barry was there for me when absolutely no living person would lend a kind ear. Although we are separated by hundreds of years and a plane of existence, we still managed to find each other. Bartholomew was married three times and fathered nine children. He may have died as an elderly man will illness but he appears to me as a strong lad that still has many years to live and I am eternally grateful to be his friend."

I placed the wreath in it's prop and tucked the prop as close as I could to the tombstone. As I was speaking my eyes stayed on the grave marker to give Barry privacy. In my experience, the visiting spirit doesn't like to be monitored while attending their own vigil.

I glanced around us quickly. The sun was starting to set and the spirits of the graveyard were stirring. There was a woman ghost that has been watching us since we arrived. She kept her distance but I could tell she was very curious about us. Her long flowing white nightgown moved with the wind. The other color that representing its self in her apparition is her long red hair. She was so clear to me I almost thought she was a tangible person but my friends never once glanced in her direction.

There was now a group of ghastly soldiers from the first world war discussing the strange light coming from my being. They were approaching quickly as a unit. A group of ghost children laughed and played amongst the gravestones. One little girl was being chased by a woman that I sensed was her mother. Even after death the woman was keeping a close eye on her child.

"You need to go," Barry whispered to me discreetly.

"We going to Isabelle's or Tryon's Gastro Pub?" Lexi asked, breaking the silence amongst the living, "I'm starving."

"I haven't been to Tryon's in a while. Pheebs and I went to Isabelle's on Monday," I started moving to the gate making sure not to glance behind me as I went. The large groups of ghosts were starting to cross pollinate discussing the strange light they saw within me. Barry stayed back to make sure we weren't being followed.

"Margarita Monday cannot be missed!" Pheobe proclaimed.

"I'm fine with the pub," Khai said, ignoring Pheobe's outburst, pulling me closer to their side as we walked.

"I could go for some thick cut fries and a fancy burger. They have one of my favorite beers on tap too," I agreed, "Let's go."

Check out other books by this Author!

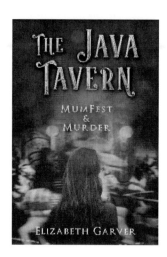 

THE JAVA TAVERN SERIES:

Book 1: Fangs & Fiends
Book 2: Mumfest & Murder
Book 3: Blood Moon Sacrifice
Book 4: *Coming soon!*

Don't forget to follow the series on Instagram and Facebook!

About the Author

Elizabeth Garver lives in New Bern, North Carolina with her husband and two kids. In her spare time, Elizabeth likes to go to the beach, create art and study the dark arts. Elizabeth has worked in customer service at various professions including local radio, construction, retail, live-in nanny, and customer service weaved throughout but writing has always been her main passion. Elizabeth has been moonlighting as a fantasy writer since the conception of the internet. On the internet, she is known as #DrunkBeth and you can learn more about her and future projects on drunkbeth.com

Made in United States
North Haven, CT
27 November 2022

27254425R00159